"You Weren't A Virgin By Accident."

She colored. "I don't date much…."

Kemp waved away the rest of the reply. "You're in love with me. I've always known it. There isn't any other reason that would make you give yourself to a man without marriage."

He moved closer, taking her gently by the shoulders. "You'll work for me until we find out, one way or another, if there are going to be any consequences."

"I should never have…!"

"We're both human." He searched her eyes. "I love the way you were with me," he added huskily. "Try not to be ashamed of something so beautiful."

He was saying something incredible. She stared up at him, fascinated.

"I was happy being alone until you came along and shook up my life," he murmured, watching her closely. "I can't go back."

Dear Reader,

It's November and perhaps the weather is turning a bit cooler where you are…so why not heat things up with six wonderful Silhouette Desire novels? *New York Times* bestselling author Diana Palmer is back this month with a LONG, TALL TEXANS story not to be missed. You've loved Blake Kemp and his ever-faithful assistant, Violet, in other books…. Now you finally get their love story, in *Boss Man*.

Heat continues to generate in DYNASTIES: THE ASHTONS with Laura Wright's contribution, *Savor the Seduction*. Grant and Anna shared a night of passion some months ago…now he's wondering if they have a shot at a repeat performance. And the temperature continues to rise as Sara Orwig delivers her share of surprises, in *Highly Compromised Position*, the latest installment in the TEXAS CATTLEMAN'S CLUB: THE SECRET DIARY series. (Hint, someone in Royal, Texas, is pregnant!)

Brenda Jackson gets things simmering in *The Chase Is On*, another fabulous Westmoreland story with a strong emphasis on food…tasty! And Bronwyn Jameson is back with the conclusion of her PRINCES OF THE OUTBACK series. Who wouldn't want to share body heat with *The Ruthless Groom*? Last but not least, get all hot and bothered in the boardroom with Margaret Allison's business-becomes-pleasure holiday story, *Mistletoe Maneuvers*.

Here's hoping you find plenty of ways to keep yourself warm. Enjoy all we have to offer at Silhouette Desire.

Best,

Melissa Jeglinski

Melissa Jeglinski
Senior Editor
Silhouette Books

Please address questions and book requests to:
Silhouette Reader Service
U.S.: 3010 Walden Ave., P.O. Box 1325, Buffalo, NY 14269
Canadian: P.O. Box 609, Fort Erie, Ont. L2A 5X3

DIANA PALMER

BOSS MAN

Published by Silhouette Books

America's Publisher of Contemporary Romance

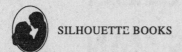 SILHOUETTE BOOKS

ISBN 0-373-76688-2

BOSS MAN

Copyright © 2005 by Diana Palmer

Visit Silhouette Books at www.eHarlequin.com

Printed in U.S.A.

DIANA PALMER

has a gift for telling the most sensual tales with charm and humor. With over 40 million copies of her books in print, Diana Palmer is one of North America's most beloved authors and considered one of the top ten romance authors in America.

Diana's hobbies include gardening, archaeology, anthropology, iguanas, astronomy and music. She has been married to James Kyle for over twenty-five years, and they have one son.

One

Violet Hardy sat at her desk and wondered why she'd ever taken this secretarial job in the first place. Her boss, Jacobsville, Texas, attorney Blake Kemp, didn't appreciate her at all. She'd only been trying to keep him from dying of a premature heart attack by changing his regular coffee to decaf. For her pains, she'd been on the receiving end of the worst insult she could ever imagine, and from the one man in the world that she loved above all others. She knew her co-workers were as upset as she was. They'd been kindness itself. But nothing made up for the fact that Blake Kemp thought Violet was fat.

She looked down at her voluptuous body in a purple dress with a high neckline, frilly bodice and straight skirt, vaguely aware that the style did nothing for her. She would be wearing it today, of all days, when Kemp gave her that disapproving scrutiny. Her mother had tried to tell her, gently, that frills and big bosoms didn't match. Worse, a tight-fitting skirt only emphasized those wide hips.

She'd been trying so hard to lose weight. She'd given up sweets, joined a gym, and worked hard at cooking regular and weight-conscious meals for herself and her elderly mother, who had a heart condition. Her father had died the year before of an apparent heart attack. But just lately there were rumors that her co-worker Libby Collins's stepmother might be responsible for Mr. Hardy's sudden death. Janet Collins had been suspected of poisoning an elderly man in a nursing home, and she'd taken Mr. Hardy for quite a sum of money before he died unexpectedly, just after being seen with her in a motel room. It had been too late for Mrs. Hardy to stop payment on the check, because she didn't realize the money was missing until well after the funeral.

Violet and her mother had been devastated, not only by his loss, but by the disastrous financial condition he'd left behind. They'd lost their nest egg, their home, their car, everything. The woman who'd convinced Mr. Hardy to give her a quarter of a million dollars couldn't be positively identified. And she'd run up accounts in department stores and even jewelry stores for which Mr. Hardy's estate was suddenly responsible. Her mother had had the first stroke just after the funeral. Violet's small, separate inheritance had been just enough to support them for a few months. But after it ran out, Violet had been forced to support them both. There had been a vacancy at Kemp's office, working with Libby Collins and Mabel Henry. Fortunately, Violet had taken a business course in spite of her father's disapproval. She'd never have to get a job, he'd said confidently.

It was nice working in Kemp's office and she was a good secretary. But her boss didn't appreciate her. Less today than ever before. She raged for five minutes, while her helpless co-workers listened and sympathized. She poured out her heart, including her feelings for her taciturn boss.

"Don't take it so much to heart, dear," Mabel said finally, sympathizing with her despair. "We all have bad days."

"He thinks I'm fat," Violet said miserably.

"He didn't say anything."

"Well, you know how he looked at me and what he insinuated," Violet muttered, glaring down the hall.

Mabel grimaced. "He's had a bad day."

"So have I," Violet said flatly.

Libby Collins patted her on the shoulder. "Buck up, Violet," she said gently. "Just give it a couple of days and he'll apologize. I'm sure he will."

Violet wasn't sure. In fact, she'd have bet money that an apology was the last thing on her boss's mind.

"We'll see," she replied as she went back to her desk. But she didn't believe it.

She pushed back her long dark hair and her blue eyes were tearful, although she was careful to conceal her hurt feelings. It was far worse than just his insinuation that she was overweight. She'd overheard Mabel and Libby whispering that the intercom had been on when Violet had poured out her heart to her co-workers after Kemp's blistering attack over the decaffeinated coffee he'd been given. She was crazy about him. He'd heard that. How was she ever going to be able to face him again?

It was as bad as she feared. All day, he walked out to the front to meet clients, talk about appointments and get coffee. Every single time he walked in, he glared at Violet as if she were responsible for the seven deadly sins. She began to cringe when she heard his footsteps coming down the hall.

By the end of the day, Tuesday, she knew she couldn't stay with him anymore. It was too humiliating all the way around. She was going to have to leave.

Libby and Mabel noticed her unusual solemnity. It got worse when she pulled a typed sheet from her printer, got up, took a deep breath, and walked down the hall to Kemp's office.

Seconds later, they heard him. "What the hell...?"

Violet came stalking back down the hall, red-faced and un-
nerved, with an enraged Kemp, minus his glasses, two steps
behind, waving the sheet of paper at her back.

"You can't give me one day's notice!" he raged. "I have
cases pending. You're responsible for sorting them out and
notifying the petitioners…!"

She whirled, eyes flashing. "All that information is in the
computer, along with the phone numbers! Libby knows what
to do, she's had to help me keep track of your cases when I
had to be home with Mother during her last stroke! Please
don't pretend it matters who's doing the typing or making the
phone calls, because I know it doesn't matter to you! I'm
going to work for Duke Wright!"

He was seething, but he went suddenly quiet. "Going over
to the enemy, then, Miss Hardy?"

"Mr. Wright is less excitable than you are, sir, and he
won't rage about coffee. In fact," she said audaciously, "he
makes his own!"

He looked for a retort, couldn't think up one, mashed his
sensuous lips together, let out a word under his breath that
could have had him up for charges of harassment, and
stomped back down the hall still clutching the single sheet
of paper. As an afterthought, he slammed his door.

Libby and Mabel tried not to laugh. Mr. Kemp had thrown
two people out of the office onto the sidewalk in less than a
month. His temper had gone from bad to worse, and poor Violet had caught the worst of it. Now she was leaving and it
would be lonely without her. Sadly, Libby thought, her own
workload had just doubled.

Violet apologized to her co-workers, but insisted that she
couldn't take the working situation anymore. At the end of
the day, she closed down her computer, noting that Mabel and
Libby were both out the door before she could get her things

together. Libby had already agreed to come back as soon as she had a bite to eat and finish up two cases that Kemp was presenting the next day. Violet would have offered to do it; poor Libby had problems of her own with her horrible stepmother trying to sell the Collins house out from under Libby and her brother, Curt. But Libby insisted she didn't mind.

Violet shouldered into her long sweater-jacket just as Kemp came stalking down the hall, still in a temper, his pale blue eyes flashing behind his glasses, his lean face taut with anger, his dark wavy hair slightly mussed in back from his restless fingers.

He stopped and glared at her. "I hope I've made my point about the coffee," he said bluntly. "Have you reconsidered your impulsive resignation, by the way?"

She swallowed. He'd made his point about a lot of things. She drew herself up to her full height and faced him bravely. "I have not. I'll be leaving as soon as you can get a replacement, Mr. Kemp."

His eyebrows arched. "Running away, Miss Hardy?" he asked sarcastically.

"You can call it that if you like," she replied.

His eyes glittered, angered all out of proportion by the reply. "In that case, you can consider this your last day and forget the measly notice. I'll get Libby to finish your work and I'll mail your two weeks' pay to you. If that's satisfactory."

Her face felt tight and uncomfortable at the taunting question, but she stood her ground. "That will be fine, Mr. Kemp. Thank you."

He glared at her. He was furious that he couldn't get a rise out of her. "Very well. Your office key, please."

She fumbled it off her key chain and handed it to him, careful not to let her fingers touch his. Her heart was going to break in two when the shock wore off. But she was too proud to let him see how devastated she was.

He stared down at her dark head of hair as she placed the key in his fingers. He felt an unfamiliar, uncomfortable surge of loss. He couldn't understand why. He had little to do with women these days, although he was only thirty-six. He'd lost the woman he loved years ago and had never had any inclination to risk his heart again.

Violet, however, threatened his freedom. She had a sort of empathy with people that was disturbing. She was easily hurt. He could see that this was killing her, being tipped out of his office, out of his life. But he had to let her go. She'd already gotten too close. He never wanted to feel again the pain of having his heart ripped out with the loss of a woman. His fiancée had died. He was through with love. So Violet had to go.

It was for the best, he told himself firmly. She was only infatuated with him. She'd get over it. He thought of how much she'd lost in the past year: her father, her home, her whole way of life. Now she had her invalid mother to care for, a burden she shouldered without a word of complaint. Now she had no job. He winced as he sensed the pain she must be feeling.

"It's for the best," he muttered uncomfortably.

She looked up at him, her blue eyes tragic in her rounded face. "It is?"

His jaw tautened. "You're confused about your feelings. You're only infatuated, Violet," he said as kindly as he could, watching her face flush violently. "It isn't love eternal, and there are eligible men elsewhere. You'll get over it."

Her lips actually trembled as she tried to find a comeback to that devastating revelation. She'd been afraid he'd overheard her confession of love, now she knew he had. His words made her feel like sinking into the floor. It was the worst humiliation she could ever remember feeling in her life. He couldn't possibly have made his own feelings any clearer.

"Yes, sir," she bit off, turning away. "I'll get over it."

She picked up her bits and pieces and moved toward the door. Predictably, he went to open it for her, a gentleman to the bitter end.

"Thank you," she choked, her eyes averted.

"Are you certain that Duke Wright will hire you?" he asked abruptly.

She didn't even look at him. "What do you care, Mr. Kemp?" she asked in a dull, miserable tone. "I'm out of your hair."

She walked toward her car with her heart around her ankles. Behind her, a tall man stood watching, brooding, as she walked out of his life.

She'd forgotten the cake. She'd promised to drop it by the Hart ranch for Tess, but it was still sitting in Kemp's office. She no longer had a key, and she'd rather have died than phoned him to let her in to get the cake. He'd think it was a ruse, so that she could see him again.

She stopped by the bakery instead and got another cake. Luckily for her, Tess didn't want a message on it, just the cake. She stopped by the Hart ranch property at Tess and Cag's enormous house and handed it off to their housekeeper, with a beaming smile that never reached her eyes. Then she went home.

Her mother was lying on the sofa, watching the last of her soap operas. "Hello, sweetheart," she said, smiling. "Did you have a nice day?"

"Very nice," Violet lied, smiling back. "How about you?"

"I've done very well. I made supper!"

"Mama, you aren't supposed to exert yourself," Violet protested, gritting her teeth.

"Cooking isn't exertion. I do love it so," the older woman

replied, her blue eyes that were so like Violet's sparkling with pleasure. Her hair was silver now, short and wavy. She lay on the sofa in an old gown and housecoat, her feet in socks. Nights were still chilly, even though it was April.

"Want to eat in here on trays?" Violet offered.

"That would be lovely. We can watch the news."

Violet grimaced. "Not the news," she groaned. "Something pleasant!"

"Then what would you like to watch? We've got lots of DVDs," her mother added.

Violet named a comedy about a crocodile who ate people living around a lake.

Her mother gave her an odd look. "My, my. Usually when you want to watch that one, you've had an argument with Mr. Kemp." She was fishing.

Violet cleared her throat. "We did have a little tiff," she confessed, not daring to tell her mother that the family bread-winner was temporarily out of work.

"It will all blow over," Mrs. Hardy promised. "He's a difficult man, I imagine, but he's been very kind to us. Why, when I had to go to the hospital last time, he drove you there and even sat with you until they got me over the crisis."

"Yes, I know," Violet replied, without adding that Mr. Kemp would do that for anybody. It didn't mean anything, except that he had a kind heart.

"And then there was that huge basket of fruit he sent us at Christmas." The older woman was still talking.

Violet was on her way to her bedroom to change into jeans and a sweatshirt. She wondered how she was going to get another job without naming Mr. Kemp as a reference. He might give her one. She just hated having to ask him to. She'd told her co-workers, and Kemp, that she was going to work for Duke Wright, but it had been a lie to save face.

"Going to the gym tonight?" her mother asked when she

reappeared and rifled through the DVD stack for the movie she wanted.

"Not tonight," Violet replied with a smile. Maybe never again, she was thinking. What use was it to revamp herself when she'd never see Mr. Kemp again, anyway?

Later, she cried herself to sleep, hating her own show of weakness. Fortunately, nobody else would see it. By dawn, she was up and dressed, her makeup on, her resolve firm. She was going to get a new job. She had skills. She was a hard worker. She would be an asset to any prospective employer. She told herself these things firmly, because her ego was badly hurt. She'd show Mr. Kemp. She could get a job anywhere!

Actually, that wasn't quite the case. Jacobsville was a small town. There weren't that many office jobs available, because most people lucky enough to get them worked in the same place until they retired.

There was one hope. Duke Wright, a local rancher who had a real verbal war going with Mr. Kemp, couldn't keep a secretary. He was hard, cold, and demanding. At least one secretary had left his employment in tears. His wife had left him, along with their young son, and filed for divorce. He consistently refused to sign the final papers, which had led to a furious confrontation between himself and Blake Kemp. The fistfight escalated until Chief of Police Cash Grier had to step in and break it up. Duke threw a punch at Cash, missed the chief and landed in jail. There was certainly no love lost between Duke Wright and Blake Kemp.

With that idea in mind, and gathering up her courage, she phoned him from home the next morning while her mother was still asleep.

His deep voice was easily recognizable the instant he spoke.

"Mr.…Mr. Wright? It's Violet Hardy," she stammered.

There was a surprised pause. "Yes, Miss Hardy?" he replied.

"I was wondering if you needed any secretarial help right now," she blurted out, embarrassed almost to tears just to ask the question.

There was another pause and then a chuckle. "Have you and Kemp parted ways?" he asked at once.

She felt her cheeks redden. "In fact, yes, we have," she said flatly. "I quit."

"Great!"

"Ex-excuse me?" she stammered, surprised.

"I can't get a secretary who doesn't see me as a matrimonial prospect," he told her.

"I certainly won't," she replied without thinking. "Uh, sorry!"

"Don't apologize. How soon can you get out here?"

"Fifteen minutes," she said brightly.

"You're hired. Come in right away. Be sure and tell Kemp who you're working for, will you?" he added. "It would make my day!"

She laughed. "Yes, sir. And thank you very much! I'll work hard, I'll do overtime, anything you want! Well, within reason."

"No need to worry, I'm off women for life," he said in a rough tone. "See you soon, Violet."

He hung up before she could reply. She had a job! She didn't have to tell her mother she was out of work and they wouldn't be able to afford rent payments and her car payment and food. It was such a relief that she sat staring at the phone blankly until she remembered that she had to go to work.

"I'll be home just after five, Mama," she told her mother gently, bending to kiss her forehead. It felt clammy. She frowned, standing erect. "Are you okay?"

Her mother opened pale blue eyes and managed a smile. "Just a little headache, darling, certainly nothing to worry about. I'd tell you. Honest."

Violet relaxed, but only a little. She loved her mother. Mrs. Hardy was the only person in the whole world who loved her. She had frequent unspoken terrors about losing her. It was scary.

"I'm okay!" her mother emphasized.

"You stay in bed today and don't get up and start trying to do cordon bleu in the kitchen. Okay?"

Mrs. Hardy reached out and caught Violet's hand. "I don't want to be a burden on you, darling," she said softly. "That was never what I intended."

"You can't help having a bad heart," she insisted.

"I wish I could. Your father might still be alive, if he hadn't been forced to…to go to another woman…for—" She broke off, tears brightening her eyes.

"Mama, you can't blame yourself for something you couldn't help," Violet told her, privately thinking that if she'd been married to the same man for twenty-five years and he had a stroke, she certainly wouldn't be running around on him while he was fighting just to stay alive. Her father hadn't really loved her mother, and it showed to everybody except Mrs. Hardy. The older woman was forever doing things to help other people. Until her illness, she'd always been active in the community, baking for fund-raising sales, working in her church group, taking food to bereaved families—anything she could do. Her father, a very successful Certified Public Accountant, went to work and came home and watched television. He had no sense of compassion. In fact, his mind was forever on himself, and what he needed. He and Violet had never been close, although he hadn't been a bad father, in his way.

But she couldn't say all that to her mother. Instead she bent and kissed her mother's temple again. "I love you. It's no burden to take care of you. And I mean that," she added, smiling.

"You tell that Mr. Kemp that I'm very proud he gave you the job. I don't know what we'd have done…"

Violet sat down beside her mother. "Listen, I have to tell you something."

"You're getting married?" the older woman asked hopefully, with bright eyes and a smile. "He's finally realized you're in love with him?!"

"He's realized it," Violet said, tight-lipped. "And he said I'd get over it quicker if I was working for somebody else."

Her mother's jaw fell. "And he seemed like such a nice man!" she exclaimed.

She held the other woman's hand hard. "I've got a new job," she said at once, before her mother could start worrying. "I'm going to start this morning." She smiled. "It's going to be great!"

"Start where? Working for whom?"

"Duke Wright."

Her mother's thin eyebrows arched and a twinkle came into her eyes. "He doesn't like Mr. Kemp."

"And vice versa," Violet stated firmly. "It will pay just as well as Mr. Kemp did," she added, mentally crossing her fingers, "and he won't complain about how I make coffee."

"Excuse me?" Mrs. Hardy asked.

Violet cleared her throat. "Never mind, Mama. It's going to be fine. I like Mr. Wright."

Mrs. Hardy pressed her hand again. "If you say so. I'm sorry, darling. I know how you feel about Mr. Kemp."

"Since he doesn't feel the same way, it's for the best if I don't go on working there and eating my heart out over him," Violet said realistically. "I daresay I'll find other company, someone who doesn't think I'm too fat…" She stopped at once and flushed.

Her mother looked furious. "You are not fat! I can't believe Mr. Kemp had the audacity to say something like that to you!"

"He didn't," Violet replied at once. "He just…insinuated it." She sighed. "He's right. I am fat. But I'm trying so hard to lose weight!"

Her mother held her hand tighter. "Listen to me, darling," she said softly. "A man who really cares about you isn't going to dwell on what he considers faults. Your father used that same argument to me," she added unexpectedly. "He actually said that he went to that other woman because she was slender and well-groomed."

"He…did?"

She grimaced. "I should have told you. Your father never loved me, Violet. He was in love with my best friend and she married somebody else. He married me to get even with her. He wanted a divorce two months later, but I was pregnant with you, and in those days, people really gossiped about men who walked out on a pregnant wife. So we stayed together and tried to make a home for you. Looking back," she said wearily, lying back down on her pillows, "perhaps I made a mistake. You don't know what a good marriage is, do you? Your father and I hardly ever did anything together, even when you were little."

Violet pushed back her mother's disheveled hair. "I love you very much," she told her parent. "I think you're wonderful. So do a lot of other people. It was my father's loss if he couldn't see how special you were."

"At least I have you" came the soft reply, with a smile. "I love you, too, darling."

Violet fought tears. "Now I really have to go," she said. "I can't afford to lose my new job before I start it!"

Her mother laughed. "You be careful!"

"I'll drive under the speed limit," she promised.

"Mr. Wright isn't married now, is he?" Mrs. Hardy wondered.

"Yes, he is. He refused to sign the final divorce papers." She laughed. "That's why he had the fight with Mr. Kemp."

"Is it spite, do you think, or does he still love her?"

"Everybody thinks he still loves her, but she's making a fortune working as a lawyer in New York City and she doesn't want to come back here."

"They have a little boy. Doesn't she think his father has any right to see the child?"

"They're still arguing about custody."

"What a pity."

"People should think hard about having children," Violet said with conviction, "and they shouldn't ever be accidents."

"That's just what I've always said," Mrs. Hardy replied. "Have a good day, darling."

"You, too. The phone's right here and I'm going to write down Mr. Wright's number in case you need me." She penciled it on the pad next to the phone, smiled, and went to get her purse.

Duke Wright lived in a huge white Victorian house. Local gossip said that his wife had wanted it since she was a child, living in a poor section of Jacobsville. She'd married Duke right out of high school and started to college after the honeymoon was over. College had opened a new world to her eyes. She'd decided to study law, and Duke stood by and let her have her way, sure that she'd never want to leave Jacobsville. But she got a taste of city life when she went on to law school in San Antonio, and she decided to work in a law firm there.

Nobody understood exactly why they decided to have a child in her first year as a practicing estate lawyer. She didn't seem happy about it, although she had the child. But a live-in nurse had to be employed because Mrs. Wright spent more and more time at the office. Then, two years ago, she'd been offered a position in a well-known law firm in New York City and she'd jumped at the chance. Duke had argued, cajoled, threatened, to try to get her to turn it down. Nothing worked. In a fit of rage, she moved out, with their son, and filed for divorce. Duke had fought it tooth and nail. Just this month, she'd presented him with divorce papers, demanding his signature, which also required him to remit full custody of his five-year-old son to her. He'd gone wild.

To look at him, though, Violet thought, he seemed very self-possessed and confident. He was tall and bronzed with a strong face, square chin, deep-set dark eyes and blondish-brown hair which he wore conventionally cut. He had the physique of a rodeo star, which he'd been before his father's untimely death and his switch from cowboy to cattle baron. He ran purebred red angus cattle, well-known in cattle circles for their pedigree. He had all the scientific equipment necessary for a prosperous operation, including high-tech methods of genetic breeding, artificial insemination, embryo transplantation, cross-breeding for leanness, low birth weight and daily weight gain ratio, as well as expert feed formulation. He had the most modern sort of operation, right down to lagoon management and forage improvement. He had the most modern computers money could buy, and customized software to keep up with his cattle. But his newest operation was organic ham and bacon that he raised on his ranch and marketed over the Internet.

Violet was staggered at the high-tech equipment in the office he maintained on his sprawling ranch outside town.

"Intimidated?" he drawled, smiling. "Don't worry. It's easier to use than it looks."

"Can you operate it all?" she asked, surprised.

He shrugged. "With the average duration of secretarial assistance around here, I have to be able to do things myself," he said heavily. He gave her a long look and stuck his lean hands in the pockets of his jeans. "Violet, I'm not an easy boss," he confessed. "I have moods and rages, and sometimes I blow up when things upset me. You'll need nerves of steel to last long here. So I won't blame you if you have reservations."

Her eyebrows arched. "I worked for Blake Kemp for over a year."

He chuckled, understanding her very well. "They say he's worse than me," he agreed. "Okay. If you're game, we'll give it two weeks. After that, you can decide if it's worth the money. That's another thing," he added, smiling. "I pay better than Kemp." He named a figure that made Violet look shocked. He nodded. "That's to make it worth the aggravation. Come on, and I'll show you around the equipment."

It was fascinating. She'd never seen anything like the tangle of spreadsheets and software that ran his empire. Even the feed was mixed by computer.

"Not that you'll have to concern yourself with the organic pork operation," he added quickly. "I have three employees who do nothing except that. But these figures—" he indicated the spreadsheet "—are urgent. They have to be maintained on a daily basis."

"All of them?" she exclaimed, seeing hours and hours of overtime in statistics before her.

"Not by hand," he replied. "All the cowboys are computer literate, even the old-timers. They feed the information into handheld computers and send it to the mainframe by internal modem, right from the pastures," he told her.

She just shook her head. "It's incredible," she replied. "I hope I'm smart enough to learn all this, Mr. Wright."

He smiled approvingly. "There's nothing I appreciate

more than modesty, Miss Hardy," he replied. "You'll do fine. Ready to get started?"

"Yes, sir!" she replied.

It was a short day, mainly because she was so busy trying to learn the basics of Duke Wright's agricultural programs. She liked him. He might have a bad reputation, and she knew he could be hard to get along with, but he had saving graces.

She managed not to think about Mr. Kemp all afternoon, until she got home.

Her mother smiled at her from the sofa, where she was watching her daily soap operas. "Well, how did it go?" she asked.

"I like it!" Violet told her with a big smile. "I really do. I think I'm going to work out just fine. And, besides that, I'm going to be making a lot more money. Mama, we might even be able to afford a dishwasher!"

Mrs. Hardy sighed. "That would be lovely, wouldn't it?"

Violet kicked off her shoes and sat down in the recliner next to the sofa. "I'm so tired! I'm just going to rest for a minute and then I'll see about supper."

"We could have chili and hot dogs."

Violet chuckled. "We could have a nice salad and bread sticks," she said, thinking of the calories.

"Whatever you like, dear. Oh, by the way, Mr. Kemp came by a few minutes ago."

Violet's world came crashing down around her ears. She'd hoped to not even hear his name, at least for another few days.

"What did he want?" she asked her mother.

The older woman picked up a white envelope. "To give you this." She handed it to Violet, who sat staring at it.

"Well," she murmured. "I guess it's my final pay."

Mrs. Hardy muted the television set. "Why not open it and see?"

Violet didn't want to, but her mother looked expectant. She tore open the envelope and extracted a check and a letter. With her breath in her throat, she slowly unfolded it.

"What does it say?" her mother prompted.

Violet just stared at it, unbelieving.

"Violet, what is it?"

Violet drew in a breath. "It's a letter of recommendation," she said huskily.

Two

"**I** can't believe he actually gave me one," Violet said huskily, her heart racing from just the thought that he'd backed down that far. "I didn't ask for it."

"He told me that," her mother replied. "He said that he felt really bad about the way you left, Violet, and that he hoped you'd be happy in your new job."

Violet looked up at her parent, hating herself for being so happy with these crumbs of Kemp's regard. "He did?" She caught herself. "Did you tell him where I was working?"

Mrs. Hardy shifted on the sofa. "Well, dear, he looked so pleasant and we had such a nice conversation. I thought, why upset the man?"

Violet laughed helplessly. "What did you tell him, Mother?" she asked gently.

"I said you were working in a local office for a very nice man, doing statistics," she said with a chuckle. "He didn't actually ask where. He started to, and I changed the subject. He said Libby and Mabel were splitting your work for the time being. He's going to advertise for a new secretary," she added.

Violet sighed. "I hope he's happy with whichever poor soul gets the job," she said.

"No, you don't. I know you hated to leave. But, dear, if he doesn't feel the same way, it's a blessing in the long run," her mother said wisely. "No sense eating your heart out."

"That's what I thought when I quit," Violet admitted. She got to her feet, putting the letter and check back in the envelope. "I'll go fix something to eat."

"You could make a pot of coffee," her mother suggested.

Violet gave her a glare. "You don't need to be drinking caffeine."

"Don't we have any decaf?"

It reminded Violet too much of her ex-boss, and she wasn't enthusiastic. But her mother loved coffee, and missed being able to drink it. She didn't know about the coffee wars in Kemp's office, either. Violet forced a smile. "I'll see," she said, and left her mother to the soap opera.

The first few days out of Kemp's office were the hardest. She couldn't forget how she'd looked forward to every new day, to each morning's first glimpse of her handsome boss. Her heart had jumped at the sound of his voice. She tingled all over when, rarely, he smiled at her when she finished a difficult task for him. Even the scent of a certain masculine cologne could trigger memories, because he always smelled of it. She felt deprived because her life would no longer contain even a casual glimpse of him. She was working for his worst enemy. Not much likelihood that Kemp would turn up on Duke Wright's ranch in the near or distant future.

But as time passed, Violet slowly fell into a routine at Duke's ranch. The spreadsheet programs were easy to use once she learned what the various terms meant, like weight gain ratio and birth weight. She learned that Duke used artificial insemination to improve the genetics of his cattle, selecting for low birth weight, good weight gain ratios for offspring and lean cuts of meat in the beef cattle offspring that would eventually be generated by his purebred herd sires and dams.

She was fascinated to find that science was used to predict leanness and tenderness of beef cuts, that genetics could manipulate those factors to produce a more marketable product for consumers.

She was fascinated by the various pedigrees and the amount of history contained in his breeding programs. It was like an organic history of Texas just to look back over the first herds that had contributed to Duke's formidable beef concern. He kept photographic records as well as statistical ones, and she found the early beef sires short, stocky and woolly compared to modern ones. It graphically showed the progression of genetic breeding.

Her duties were routine and hardly exciting, but she made good wages and she liked the people she worked with. Duke had full time and part-time cowboys, as well as a veterinary student who worked one semester and went to school one semester. He had three people who did nothing but work with his Internet Web site that sold his premium organic ham and bacon products.

But Violet's job was separate from that of the other workers. There was a new storefront that Duke had just opened in Jacobsville to market his organic pork. There was also a modern office complex adjacent to the enormous barn, where the production and lab staff were located. The barn, in addition to containing the pride of his purebred cattle herd, his expensive seed bulls, there was also a climate controlled room where the frozen sperm and embryos were kept for artificial insemination. The procedure itself was conducted in the barn. Purebred embryos from superior herd sires, as well as straws of semen from champion bulls who were now long dead, were kept in vats of liquid nitrogen. These were placed in surrogate mothers who might be Holsteins or even mixed breed cattle rather than the purebred heifers he also sold along with each new crop of yearling bulls from purebred sires.

Violet had a passing acquaintance with the employees who ran the lab, one of whom was a graduate biologist named Delene Crane, a young woman with a quirky sense of humor. They were nodding acquaintances, because she didn't have much free time to socialize. None of the staff did, for that matter. Routine at the ranch was chaotic because spring was the busiest time for everyone, with calves being born and recorded and branding in full swing.

She knew that Duke used not only hot branding, but also had computer chips on plastic tags that dangled from the ears of his cattle. These chips contained the complete history of each cow or bull. The information was scanned into a hand-held computer and sent by modem to Violet's computer to be compiled into the spreadsheet program.

"It's just fascinating," Violet told Duke as she watched the information updating itself on her computer screen from minute to minute.

He smiled wearily. He was dusty. His chaps and boots were dirty and blood-stained because he'd been helping with calving all day. His red shirt was wet all over. His hair, under his wide-brimmed Stetson, was dripping sweat. His leather gloves, tight-fitting and suede-colored, were dangling from the wide belt buckle at his lean waist over his jeans.

"It's taken a lot of work to get this operation so far," he confessed, his eyes on the screen as he spoke, his voice deep and pleasant in the quiet office. "And a lot of cash. I've been in the hole for the past year. But I'm just beginning to show a profit. I think the pork operation may be what finally gets me in the black."

"Where are the pigs kept?" she wondered aloud, because she'd only seen cattle and horses so far. In addition to the cattle herd, Duke maintained a small herd of purebred Appaloosa horses.

"Far enough away that they aren't easy to smell," he replied with a grin. "They have their own complex about a mile down the road. It's remarkably clean, and purely organic. They have pastures to roam and a stream that runs through it all the year, and they're fed a carefully formulated organic diet. No pesticides, no hormones, no antibiotics unless they're absolutely necessary."

"You sound like the Harts and the Tremaynes and…" she began.

"…and Cy Parks and J. D. Langley," he finished for her, chuckling. "They did give me the idea. It's catching on. Christabel and Judd Dunn jumped on the wagon last year."

"It's been very profitable for them, I hear," Violet replied. "Mr. Kemp handles all the paperwork for the Harts and Cy Parks…" She bit her tongue as his face hardened and the smile faded. "Sorry, boss," she said at once.

He moved jerkily. "No harm done."

But she knew how he felt about Kemp. She opened a second window on the computer screen and diverted him with a question about another procedure.

He explained the process to her and smiled. "You're a diplomat, Violet. I'm glad you needed a job."

"Me, too, Mr. Wright," she replied, smiling.

He pulled his hat down over his eyes. "Well, I've played hooky as long as I can," he said with a grimace. "I'll get back to work before Lance comes in here and lassos me and drags me back out to the pasture. You go home at five regardless of the phone, okay?" he added. "I know you worry about your mother. You don't need to do overtime."

"Thanks," she said, and meant it. "It's hard for her to be alone in the evening. She gets scared."

"I don't doubt it. Oh, if you get a minute," he added from the door, "call Calhoun Ballenger and tell him I'm sending him a donation for his campaign."

She grinned. "I'll be happy to do that! I'm voting for him, too."

"Good for you." He closed the door carefully behind him.

Violet made the call, finished up her work, and left on time. She had to run by the post office on the way home to put Duke's correspondence into the mail.

As luck would have it, Kemp was in the lobby when she walked in the door, having just put a last-minute letter into the outgoing post.

He stopped short when he saw her, his pale blue eyes narrow and accusing. She was keenly aware that her lipstick was long gone, that her hair was sticking out in comic angles from her once-neat braid, that one leg of her panty hose was laddered. She couldn't run into him when she looked neat and pretty, she thought miserably. To top it all off, she was wearing white jeans that were too tight and a red overblouse with ruffles that made her look vaguely clownish. She ground her teeth as she glared back at him.

"Mr. Kemp," she said politely, and started to go around him.

He stepped right into her path. "What's Wright been doing to you?" he asked. "You look worn to the bone."

Her thin eyebrows arched as she registered genuine concern in that narrow gaze. She cleared her throat. "It's roundup," she replied.

He nodded understanding. "The Harts are breaking out in

hives already," he mused, and almost smiled. "They've had some problems with their exports to Japan as well. I suppose the cattle business is wearing on the nerves."

She smiled shyly. "Everybody's rushing to record all the pertinent information for every new calf, and there are a lot of them."

"He's opened a meat shop here in town," he remarked. "It sells organic hams and sausage and bacon."

"Yes. His employees run a Web site, too, so that he can sell his pork on the Internet." She hesitated. Her heart was racing like mad and she felt her knees weakening just from the long, shared looks. She missed him so much. "How… how are Libby and Mabel?"

"Missing you." He made it sound as if she'd left him in a bind.

She shifted to the other foot. If they'd been alone, she'd have had more to say about the accusing look he was giving her. But people were coming and going all around them. "Thank you. For the recommendation, I mean."

He shrugged. "I didn't think Wright would take you on," he said honestly. "It's no secret that he hates having women around the ranch since the divorce."

"Delene Crane works with him," she replied, curious. "She's a woman."

"He's known Delene since they were in college together," he told her. "He doesn't think of her as a woman."

Interesting, she mused, because Delene wasn't a bad-looking woman. She had red hair and green eyes and a milky complexion with a few freckles. She froze out the cowboys who gave her flirting glances, though. She was also strictly business with Duke, so maybe it was true that he didn't think of her as a romantic prospect. She wondered why Delene didn't feel comfortable around men…

"How's your mother?" Kemp asked abruptly.

She grimaced. "She does things they told her not to do," she lamented. "Especially lifting heavy stuff. The doctors said that she still has a tendency toward clots, despite the blood thinners they give her. They didn't say, but I know that once a person has one or two strokes, they're almost predisposed to have more."

He nodded slowly. "But there are drugs to treat that, now. I'm sure your doctor is taking good care of her."

"He is," she had to agree.

"Your mother is special."

She smiled. "Yes. I think so, too."

He looked past her. "It's clouding up. You'd better get your letters mailed, so you don't get soaked when you leave."

"Yes." She looked at him with pain in her eyes. She loved him. It was so much worse that he knew, and pitied her for it. She glanced away, coloring faintly. "Yes, I'd better…go."

Unexpectedly, he reached out and pushed back a long strand of black hair that had escaped her braid. He tugged it behind her ear, his gaze intent and solemn as he watched her heartbeat race at her bodice. He heard her breath catch at the faint contact. He felt guilty. He could have been kinder to Violet. She had enough on her plate just with her mother to care for. She cared about him. She'd shown it, in so many ways, when she worked with him. He hadn't wanted to encourage her, or give her false hope. But she looked so miserable.

"Take care of yourself," he said quietly.

She swallowed, hard. "Yes, sir. You, too."

He moved aside to let her pass. As she went by, a faint scent of roses drifted up into his nostrils. Amazing how much he missed that scent around his office. Violet had become almost like a stick of furniture in the past year, she was so familiar. But at the same time, he was aware of an odd, tender nurturing of himself that he'd never had in his adult life. Violet made him think of open fireplaces in winter, of warm lamplight in the darkness. Her absence had only served to make him realize how alone he was.

She walked on to the mail slots, unaware of his long, aching stare at her back. By the time she finished her chore, he was already out the door and climbing into his Mercedes.

Violet watched him drive away before she opened the door of the post office and went outside. It was starting to rain. She'd get wet, but she didn't care. The odd, tender encounter made her head spin with pleasure. It would be a kind thought to brighten her lonely life.

There was a lot of talk around town about Janet Collins. She'd gone missing and Libby and Curt were the subject of a lot of gossip. Jordan Powell had been seen with Libby, but nobody took that seriously. He was also seen with old Senator Merrill's daughter, Julie, doing the social rounds. Violet wondered if Libby felt the rejection as much as Violet felt it over Kemp. Her co-worker had a flaming crush on Jordan in recent weeks, but it seemed the feeling wasn't reciprocated.

Violet's mother seemed to be weakening as the days passed. It was hard for Violet to work and not worry about her. She'd started going back to the gym on her way home from work three days a week, but it was only for a half hour at a time. She'd splurged on a cell phone and she kept it with her all the time now, just in case there was ever an emergency when she wasn't home. Her mother had a hot button on the new phone at home, too, so that she could push it and speed-dial Violet.

She had her long hair trimmed and frosted, and she actually asked a local boutique owner for tips on how to make the most of her full figure. She learned that lower cut blouses helped to diminish a full bosom. She also learned that a longer jacket flattered wide hips, and that straight lines made her look taller. She experimented with hairstyles until she found one that flattered her full face, and with makeup until she learned how to use it so that it looked natural. She was changing, growing, maturing, slimming. But all of it was a means to an end, as much as she hated to admit it. She wanted Blake Kemp to miss her, want her, ache for her when he looked at her. It was a hopeless dream, but she couldn't let go of it.

Kemp, meanwhile, spent far too much time at his home thinking about ways and means to get Violet to come back.

He stretched out on his burgundy leather couch to watch the weather channel with his two female Siamese cats, Mee and Yow, curled against his chest. Mee, a big seal-point, rarely cuddled with him. Yow, a blue-point, was in his lap the minute he sat down. He felt a kinship with the cats, who had become his family. They sat with him while he watched television at night. They curled up on the big oak desk when he worked there at his computer. Late at night, they climbed under the covers on either side of him and purred him to sleep.

The Harts thought his cat mania was a little overdone. But, then, they weren't really cat people, except for Cag and Tess. Their cats were mostly strays. Mee and Yow, on the other hand, were purebred. Blake had brought both of them home with him together from a pet store, where they'd been in cages behind glass for weeks, the last products of a cattery that had gone bankrupt. He'd felt sorry for them. More than likely, he told himself, they'd set him up. Cats were masters of the subtle suggestion. It was amazing how a fat, healthy cat could present itself as an emaciated, starving orphan. They were still playing mind tricks on him after four years of co-existence. It still worked, too.

He thought about Violet and her mother, and remembered that the elderly Mrs. Hardy was allergic to fur. Violet loved animals. She kept little figurines of cats on her desk. He'd never asked her to his home, but he was certain that she'd love his cats. He imagined she'd have Duke Wright bringing calves right up to the porch for her to pet.

His eyes flashed at the thought of Violet getting involved with the other man. Wright was bitter over the divorce and the custody suit his wife had brought against him. He blamed Kemp for it, but Kemp was only doing what any other attorney would have done in his place. If the soon-to-be ex-Mrs. Wright was as happy as she seemed in that high-powered property law job she held in New York City, she wasn't likely to ever come home. She loved the little boy as much as Duke did, and she felt it was better not to have him dangling between two parents. Kemp didn't agree. A child had two parents. It would only lead to grief to deny access to either of them.

He shook his head. What a pity that people had children before they thought about the consequences. They never improved a bad marriage. Kemp's clientele shot that truth home every time he handled a divorce case. The children were always the ones who suffered most.

Beka Wright had never admitted it, and Kemp never pried, but local gossip had it that Duke had deliberately hidden her birth control pills at a critical time, hoping that a baby would cure her of ambition. It hadn't. He was an overbearing sort of man, who expected a woman to do exactly what he told her to do. His father had been the same, a domineering autocrat whose poor wife had walked in a cold rain with pneumonia while he was out of town one January weekend in a last, fatal attempt to escape him. Death had spared her further abuse. Duke had grown up with that same autocratic attitude and assumed that it was the way a normal man dealt with his wife. He was learning to his cost that marriage meant compromise.

Blake looked around at his house with its Western motifs,

burgundy leather mingling with dark oak and cherry wood
furniture. The carpet and the curtains were earth tones. He
enjoyed a quiet atmosphere after the turmoil of his working
life. But he wondered what a woman would do with the
décor.

Mee curled her claws into his arm. He winced, and moved
them. She was sound asleep, but when she felt his hand on
her, she snuggled closer and started purring.

He laughed softly. No, he wasn't the marrying sort. He was
a gourmet cook. He did his own laundry and housework. He
could sew on a button or make a bed. Like most other ex-special forces officers, he was independent and self-sufficient.
A veteran of the first war with Iraq, he mustered out with the
rank of captain. He'd been in the Army reserves after he
graduated from law school and started practicing in Jacobsville, and his unit had been called up. He and Cag Hart had
served in the same mechanized division. Few people knew
that, because he and Cag didn't talk much about the missions
they'd shared. It forged bonds that noncombatants could not
understand.

He reached for the remote control and changed the channel. He paused on the weather channel to see when the rain was
going to stop, and then went on to the History channel, where
he spent most of his free time in the evenings. He often thought
that if he ever came across a woman who enjoyed military history, he might be coaxed into rejoining the social scene.

But then he remembered the woman he'd lost, and the
ache started all over again. He turned up the volume and
leaned back, his mind shifting to the recounting of Alexan-
der the Great's final successful campaign against the Persian
king Darius in 331 B.C. at Gaugemela.

Violet was late getting home the following Friday. She'd
stopped by the gym and then remembered that there was no

milk in the house. She'd gone by the grocery store as well. When she pulled up into the driveway of the small, rickety rental house, she found her mother sitting on the ground beside the small flower garden at the porch steps. Mrs. Hardy wasn't moving.

Panicking, Violet jumped out of her car without bothering to close the door, and ran toward her parent.

"Mama!" she screamed.

Her mother jerked, just faintly. Her blue eyes were startled as she turned her head and looked at her daughter. She was breathing heavily. But she laughed. "Darling, it's all right!" she said at once. "I just got winded, that's all! I'm all right!"

Violet knelt beside her. Tears were rolling down her cheeks. Her face was white. She was shaking.

"Oh, baby." Mrs. Hardy winced as she reached out and cuddled Violet close, whispering soft endearments. "I'm sorry. I'm so sorry. I wanted to weed my flower bed and put out those little seedlings I'd grown in the kitchen window. I just worked a little too hard, that's all. See? I'm fine."

Violet pulled back, terrified. Her mother was all she had in the world. She loved her so much. How would she go on living if she lost her mother? That fear was written all over her.

Mrs. Hardy winced when she saw it. She hugged Violet close. "Violet," she said sadly, "one day you'll have to let me go. You know that."

"I'm not ready yet," Violet sobbed.

Mrs. Hardy sighed. She kissed Violet's dark hair. "I know," she murmured, her eyes faraway as they looked toward the horizon. "Neither am I."

Later, as they sat over bowls of hot soup and fresh corn bread, Mrs. Hardy studied her daughter with concern.

"Violet, are you sure you're happy working at Duke Wright's place?" she asked.

"Of course I am," Violet said stolidly.

"I think Mr. Kemp would like it if you went back to work with him."

Violet stared at her with her spoonful of soup in midair. "Why would you say that, Mama?"

"Mabel, who works at your office, stopped by to see me at lunch. She says Mr. Kemp is so moody they can hardly work with him anymore. She said she thinks he misses you."

Violet's heart jumped. "That wasn't how he sounded when I ran into him in the post office the other day," she said. "But he was acting…oddly."

The older woman smiled over her soup spoon. "Often men don't know what they want until they lose it."

"Bring on the day." Violet laughed softly.

"So, dear, back to my first question. Do you like your new job?"

She nodded. "It's challenging. I don't have to deal with sad, angry, miserable people whose lives are in pieces. You know, I didn't realize until I changed jobs how depressing it is to work in a law office. You see such tragedies."

"I suppose cattle are a lot different."

"There's just so much to learn," Violet agreed. "It's so complex. There are so many factors that produce good beef. I thought it was only a matter of putting bulls and heifers in the same pasture and letting nature do its work."

"It isn't?" her mother asked, curious.

Violet grinned. "Want to know how it works?"

"Yes, indeed."

So Violet spent the next half hour walking her mother, hypothetically speaking, through the steps involved in creating designer beef.

"Well!" the elderly woman exclaimed. "It isn't simple at all."

"No, it isn't. The records are so complicated…"

The sudden ringing of the telephone interrupted Violet. She frowned. "It's probably another telemarketer," she muttered. "I wish we could afford one of those new answering machines and caller ID."

"One day a millionaire will walk in the front door carrying a glass slipper and an engagement ring," Mrs. Hardy ventured with a mischievous glance.

Violet laughed as she got up and went to answer the phone. "Hardy residence," she said in her light, friendly tone.

"Violet?"

It was Kemp! She had to catch her breath before she could even answer him. "Yes, sir?" she stammered.

He hesitated. "I have to talk to you and your mother. It's important. May I come over?"

Violet's mind raced. The house was a mess. She was a mess. She was wearing jeans and a shirt that didn't fit. Her hair needed washing. The living room needed vacuuming…!

"Who is it, dear?" Mrs. Hardy called.

"It's Mr. Kemp, Mama. He says he needs to speak to us."

"Isn't it nice that we have some of that pound cake left?" Mrs. Hardy wondered aloud. "Tell him to come right on, dear."

Violet ground her teeth together. "It's all right," she told Kemp.

"Fine. I'll be there in fifteen minutes." He hung up before Violet could ask him what he wanted.

She turned worriedly to her mother. "Do you think it might be something about me coming back to work for him?"

"Who can say? You should wash your hair, dear. You'll have just enough time."

"Not to do that and vacuum and pick up around the living room," she wailed.

"Violet, the chores can wait," her mother replied amusedly. "You can't. Go, girl!"

Violet turned like a zombie and went right to the bathroom to wash her hair. By the time she heard Kemp pulling up in the driveway, she had on a nice low-cut short-sleeved blue sweater and clean white jeans. Her hair was clean and she left it down, because she didn't have time to braid it. She was wearing bedroom shoes, but that wasn't going to matter, she decided.

She opened the door.

Kemp gave her a quiet going-over with his pale blue eyes. But he didn't remark about her appearance. He was scowling. "I have something to say that your mother needs to hear, but I don't want to upset her."

There went her dreams of being rehired. "What is it about?" she asked.

He drew in a sharp breath. "Violet, I want to have your father exhumed. I think Janet Collins killed him."

Three

Violet wasn't sure she was hearing right. She knew there was something going on with Janet Collins. Curt had come by her office when he carried a note to Duke from Jordan Powell, his boss. He'd told her that he and Libby were going to have to have their father exhumed because there were suspicions that Janet, their stepmother, might have killed him. She was suspected of killing at least one other elderly man by poison. Violet and her mother knew about the waitress Mr. Hardy had had his fling with. But they'd never questioned the cause of death. And they'd never found out who the waitress was. Now, a lot of questions she hadn't wanted even to ask were suddenly being answered.

Her lips parted on a husky sigh. "Oh, dear."

Kemp closed the door behind him and tilted Violet's chin up to his eyes. "I don't want to do this," he said softly. "But there's a very good chance that your father was murdered, Violet. You don't want Janet Collins to get away with it, if she's guilty. Neither do I."

"You're right," she agreed. "But what about Mama?"

He drew in a long breath. "I have to have her signature. I can't do it on yours alone."

They exchanged worried looks.

His eyes suddenly narrowed on her oval face in its frame of dark hair. Her skin was clean and bright. She wasn't wearing makeup, except a touch of pink lipstick. And that sweater… His eyes slid down to her breasts with quiet sensuality. They narrowed, as he appreciated how deliciously full-breasted she was. She had a small waist, too. The jeans emphasized the nicely rounded contours of her hips.

"I've lost weight!" she blurted out.

"Don't lose any more," he murmured absently. "You're perfect."

Her eyebrows arched. "Sir?" she stammered.

"If I weren't a confirmed bachelor, you'd make my mouth water," he replied quietly, and the eyes that met hers were steady, intent.

Her heart began racing. Her knees were weak. He wasn't blind. Any minute, he was going to notice her helpless, headlong reaction.

"But I am a confirmed bachelor," he added firmly, as much for his own benefit as for hers. "And this isn't the time, anyway. May I come in?"

"Of course." She closed the door behind him, unsettled by what he'd said.

"I planned to come by your office and tell you," he said, his voice low, "but I got caught at the last minute and by the time I finished with an upset client, you'd already left Wright's place. I'd hoped to have a little time to prepare you for what we have to do." He glanced toward the living room door. "How is she?" he asked.

She bit her lower lip. "She's had a slight spell this week," she told him worriedly. "She thinks she's stronger than she really is. Losing Daddy and finding out about his affair ruined her life."

He bit back a harsh reply. "Should we have the doctor here while I tell her?"

She sighed wearily. "I don't think it will matter." She looked up at him. "She has to know. I don't want Janet Collins to get away with murder. Neither will she. We both loved Daddy, in our way."

"All right then." He nodded for her to go ahead of him and he followed her into the room.

Her mother looked up and smiled. "Mr. Kemp! How nice to see you again!"

He smiled, pausing in front of her to shake her hand gently. "It's good to see you, too, Mrs. Hardy. But I'm afraid I may have some upsetting news."

She put down her knitting and sat up straight. "My daughter thinks I'm a marshmallow," she said with an impish look at Violet. "But I'm tougher than I look, despite my rickety blood vessels." She set her lips firmly. "You just tell me what I need to know, and I'll do what I have to."

His blue eyes twinkled. "You are a tough nut, aren't you?" he teased.

She grinned at him, looking far younger than she was. "You bet. Go on. Spill it."

His smile faded. Violet sat on the arm of her mother's chair.

"It must be bad, if you're both expecting me to keel over," she said. "It's something about Janet Collins, isn't it?"

Violet gasped. Kemp's eyebrows arched over the frames of his glasses.

"I'm not a petunia. I don't just hang on the porch all the time," Mrs. Hardy informed them. "I get my hair done, I go to the doctor's office, I see a lot of people. I know that Libby and Curt Collins are up to their ears in trouble about their stepmother, and there's a lot of talk that she's been linked to the death of an old man in a nursing home. They said she took every penny he had. And then she went on to cheat Arthur and me out of our savings, a quarter of a million dollars. It wasn't ever proven that it was her."

"I've found an eyewitness who thinks she can place Janet Collins at the motel with Arthur the last day of his life," Kemp told her, "just before the ambulance came to take him to the hospital. She ran out the door and was seen. At the hospital the doctor, not aware of any foul play, diagnosed a heart attack from the symptoms. There was no autopsy."

"That's right," Mrs. Hardy said. She gave her audience a knowing look. "And you think she killed him, don't you?" she asked Kemp.

He was impressed. "Yes, I do," he told her honestly.

"I didn't want to think about that, but I've had my doubts," she said. "He never had heart trouble. There had been some mixup at a clinic in San Antonio and he ended up getting a heart catherization that he didn't really need. What it showed was that his heart and arteries were in fine shape, no blockages at all. So it came as something of a surprise when he died only a month later of a supposed heart attack. But I was far too upset at his affair and his sudden death to think clearly."

"If it's any consolation, Janet Collins had a way with men," Kemp replied. "She was known for playing up to older men, and she isn't a bad-looking woman. Most men react predictably to a head-on assault."

Violet was wondering irrelevantly if it would work with Kemp, but she pushed that thought to the back of her mind.

"Arthur had strayed before," Mrs. Hardy said surprisingly, and with an apologetic glance at Violet. "He was a handsome, vital man, and I was always quiet and shy and rather ordinary."

"You weren't ordinary," Violet protested.

"My people were very wealthy, dear," she told her daughter sadly. "And Arthur was ambitious. He wanted his own accounting firm, and I helped him get it. Not that he didn't work hard, but he'd never have made it without my backing. I think that hurt his pride. Maybe his…affairs…were a way of proving to himself that he could still appeal to beautiful women even as he got older. I'm sorry, Violet," she added, patting her daughter's thigh. "But parents are human, too. Arthur did love you, and he tried to be a good father, even if he wasn't a good husband."

Violet clenched her teeth. She could only imagine how it would have felt to her, if she'd been married and her husband thought nothing of having affairs with other women.

"By the time Arthur started straying," Mrs. Hardy continued, "I was too fragile to leave him and strike out on my own. There was Violet, who needed both her parents and a stable environment. And I could no longer take care of myself. Arthur paid a price to stay with me, under the circumstances. I don't really blame him for what he did."

She did, though, and it showed. Violet hugged her close. "I blame him," she murmured.

"So do I," Kemp said, surprisingly firm. "Any honorable man would have asked for a divorce before getting involved with another woman."

"Why, you Puritan," Mrs. Hardy accused with a smile.

"I've got company," he jerked his thumb at Violet.

Mrs. Hardy laughed. She folded her hands in her lap. "Okay, so we've settled that Arthur probably had an affair with Janet Collins and she may have been responsible for his death. But unless he's exhumed, and an autopsy done, we can't prove it. That's why you're here, isn't it, Mr. Kemp?"

"You're amazing, Mrs. Hardy," Kemp replied with admiration in his pale blue eyes.

"I'm perceptive. Ask Violet." The smile faded. "When do you want to do it?"

"As soon as possible. I'll make the arrangements, if you're willing. There will be papers to sign. It may make news as well."

"I can manage. So can Violet," Mrs. Hardy assured him, smiling up at her daughter.

"I can," Violet assured him. "We'll both do whatever's necessary. Whatever Daddy did, she had no right to kill him."

"Very well." Kemp got up from the sofa and shook hands with Mrs. Hardy one last time. "I'll be in touch as soon as I've got things underway. You're taking this very well."

"Surprised you, did I?" The elderly woman chuckled.

He nodded. "Pleasantly, at that," he said, adding a smile. "I'll see you." He glanced at Violet. "Walk me to the door."

She got up and followed him out into the hall, her eyes wide and curious on his face.

He paused with his hand on the doorknob and looked down at her for a long moment with narrow, intent eyes.

"I'll let you know the details as soon as I work them out with the proper authorities," he told her. "You think she'll handle it all right?" he added, alluding to her mother.

"She will," Violet replied with certainty. She looked up at him with soft, hungry eyes. "How is everything at work?"

He grimaced. "I have to make the coffee myself," he muttered. "Mabel and Libby don't make it strong enough. And Mabel is ready to tear her hair out over the extra work. So I guess we'll be advertising for a new secretary."

Violet didn't notice that he had a hopeful, anticipatory look on his face, because her eyes were downcast. She thought he was criticizing her for leaving him in the lurch, and after he'd all but forced her out of his office.

She squared her shoulders. "I'm sure you'll find someone to suit you, Mr. Kemp," she said in a subdued tone.

The formality and her lack of interest irritated him. He opened the door with a jerk. "I'll be in touch," he said, and left without even looking back.

Violet closed the door behind him, forcing herself not to look hungrily at his departing back as he left. She'd hoped just for a few seconds that he might be offering her back her old job. That was obviously not the case.

Kemp climbed into his car, irritable and unsettled by Violet's lack of response when he'd practically laid her old job at her feet. Duke Wright wasn't bad-looking, and he had an eye for a pretty woman. He was all but divorced now, too. Violet was attractive. He hoped Wright wasn't trying to turn her head. He was going to check into that. For Violet's own good, of course. He wasn't interested in her himself.

Involuntarily, his mind went back eight years, to the only woman he'd really ever loved. Shannon Culbertson had been eighteen the year they started dating. It had been love at first sight for both of them. Kemp, who was already a junior partner in a local law firm, having graduated from college late at the age of twenty-eight, was in practice with Shannon's uncle. They met at the office and started dating. Within a month, they knew they were going to be married one day. Shannon had gone to a party with a girlfriend, at Julie Merrill's house. Nobody understood why Julie wanted her worst enemy at the bash, least of all Shannon—but she thought maybe Julie was willing to bury the hatchet over the rivalry of the two girls for senior president. Someone, probably Julie herself, had put a forerunner of the date rape drug into Shannon's soft drink. She had an undiagnosed heart condition, and the drug had killed her.

It still hurt Kemp to remember the aftermath. He'd mourned her for months, blamed Julie, tried to have her arrested for the crime. But her father was a state senator and wealthy. The case never got to trial, despite Kemp's best efforts.

He still resented the Merrills. He missed Shannon. But since Violet had come to work for him, he'd thought less and less about his old love. In the mornings, he'd looked forward to Violet's smiling, happy face in his office. He was afraid of the feeling he got when she nurtured him. He didn't ever want to risk loving someone again. Tragedy had hallmarked his life. He'd had a sister, Dolores, who'd died in a swimming accident his senior year of high school. His mother had died of cancer soon afterward. There had only been the two of them, because his father had gone overseas to work for an oil company in the Middle East when he was only a child, fallen in love with a French woman, and divorced his mother. He had no contact with his father. He had no interest in him.

The experiences of his life had taught him that love was dangerous, and so was getting too used to people. Violet was still infatuated with him, but she'd get over it, he told himself firmly. Better to let her go. She was young and impressionable. She'd find someone else. Perhaps Duke Wright…

His teeth clenched hard on the thought. It was strangely uncomfortable to think of Violet in some other man's arms. Very uncomfortable.

Violet looked up from her typing one morning at the sound of approaching voices, and was surprised to find Curt Collins, Libby Collins's brother, standing at her desk.

"Curt's just joined the operation, Violet," Duke Wright told her with a grin. "We've stolen him from Jordan Powell."

"It wasn't much of a steal," Curt drawled with a grim smile. "I quit my job. Jordan's changed lately."

"Curt's going to help with the cattle operation," Duke told Violet. "If he needs any information, you can give it directly to him without having to ask me first," he added with a smile.

"Okay," she agreed.

"Come on, Curt, I'll show you around the rest of the operation," the older cattleman beckoned.

"See you later, Violet," Curt murmured.

She nodded, smiling. She watched them leave, frowning. Libby was crazy about Jordan Powell, and Curt had worked for him for years. What in the world was going on?

Curt came by just as she was getting her things together. "I suppose you're wondering how I landed here," he said.

She nodded. "It's a bit of a surprise," she replied.

"Have you talked to Kemp lately?"

Her heart jumped just at the sound of his name, but she recovered quickly. "No. I haven't spoken to him for a week or two, I guess."

"There's been some unpleasantness, shall we say, between Libby and Julie Merrill."

Violet looked blank. "I wasn't aware that they even knew each other," she replied.

"They're not even acquaintances," Curt agreed. "But Julie wants Jordan, and Libby was getting in the way."

"I see."

"Anyway, Julie attacked Libby and Jordan didn't stand up for her. Jordan made some nasty remarks to Libby." He shrugged. "I'm not working for any man who bad-mouths my sister."

"I don't blame you one bit. Poor Libby!"

"She can take care of herself on good days," he said. "But Julie has some unsavory friends. Sadly for her, she walked into Kemp's office while Libby was there."

"Excuse me?"

He smiled. "You don't know, do you? There's bad blood between Kemp and Julie. She had a party at her house eight years ago and invited Shannon Culbertson, who was all but engaged to Kemp at the time. There was a rivalry between Shannon and Julie for a class office at school. Somebody put something in Shannon's drink. She died. Julie got the office."

"She was poisoned?" Violet exclaimed, fascinated by this private look at her taciturn boss's life. So he had a woman in his past after all. Was that why he didn't have much to do with women now? It made her sad to think there was another woman in his life, even a ghost. How could a living woman compete with a perfect memory?

"She wasn't poisoned. She had a hidden heart condition," he corrected. "Anyway, she died. Kemp never got over it. He did his best to have Julie tried for it, but her father had plenty of money and plenty of influence. It was listed as a tragic accident with no explanation, and the case was closed. Kemp would hang Julie if he could ever find an excuse to get her in court." He leaned forward. "Just between you and me, that might happen. Senator Merrill got busted for drunk driving. Now he and his nephew the mayor are trying to get the arresting officers fired—and Chief Cash Grier, too."

Violet's mind had to jump-shift back to the subject at hand. She was still taking in Kemp's secret past, one that she hadn't even expected. "That'll be the day, when Chief Grier will let his officers go down the drain without a fight."

"Exactly what most of us think," Curt said. "Grier is hell on drug traffickers. Which brings to mind one other rumor that's going around—that Julie has her finger in a nasty white powder distribution network."

Violet whistled. "Some news!"

"Keep it to yourself, too," he admonished. "But the point of the thing is, I was without a job and Duke said I could work for him."

"Welcome aboard, as one refugee to another."

"That's right, you and Kemp had a mixer, too, didn't you?" He smiled wryly. "Libby told me," he added when she looked surprised. "But I heard it from three other people as well. You don't keep secrets in a town like Jacobsville. We're all one big family. We know all about each other."

She smiled. "I suppose we do."

"How's your mother taking the exhumation?"

The smile faded. "She says it's not bothering her, but I know it is. She's very old-fashioned about things like that."

He looked angry. "We feel the same way. But we had to let them exhume Dad, too. Nobody wants Janet to walk away from another murder."

"That's how Mama and I feel," Violet agreed. "But it really is hard. Have you heard anything yet?"

He shook his head. "They say the results will take time. The state crime lab is backed up, so it won't be a quick process. That will make it worse, I guess."

She nodded. "But we'll get through it, won't we?" she added.

He smiled at her determination. "You bet we will."

Blake Kemp was fuming. He'd been so busy with work that he'd forgotten the exhumations until Libby had actually asked him about them. He'd promised her that he'd get right on it. But the disturbing news had nothing to do with possible murders. It had to do with the fact that Curt Collins, Libby's brother, was taking Violet to Calhoun Ballenger's volunteer staff meeting at his ranch on the following Saturday.

He'd been worried about Violet letting Duke Wright turn her head, and here she was going on a date with a very eligible, upstanding member of a founding family of Jacobsville, Texas. Even Kemp couldn't claim descent from old John Jacobs himself. Duke might have a lot of warts, but Curt was a fine young man with a promising future. And Violet was going to date him.

He didn't understand his own violent opposition to that pairing. Violet was nothing to him, after all. She was just his ex-secretary. He had no right to care if she had a private life.

But he did care. The thought of her with Curt made him uneasy. He knew Calhoun Ballenger from years past. He frequently handled cases for him. He admired and respected the local feedlot owner. There was no reason he couldn't get himself invited to that meeting. He just wanted to make sure Violet didn't do something stupid, like falling into Curt's arms at the first opportunity. It was his duty to protect her. Sort of. He picked up the phone and dialed Calhoun's number, refusing to consider his motives in any personal way.

The meeting was riotous. There were people gathered around the big recreation room that Kemp hadn't seen face-to-face in years. Some were frankly a surprise, because at least two of the county's biggest Republican contributors were in the front row.

"Interesting, isn't it?" Police Chief Cash Grier asked him with a grin, noting the direction Kemp was staring. "Ballenger's crossing party lines all over the place. He's well-known in cattlemen's circles, and locally he's the original hometown boy who came out of poverty to become a millionaire. He did it without any under-the-table dealings as well, I hear."

"That's right," Kemp told him. "Calhoun and his brother, Justin, were the poorest kids around. They made their fortunes honestly. They both married well, too."

"Calhoun's wife was his ward, they say," Grier mused.

"Yes, and Justin married a direct descendant of Big John Jacobs, the founder of Jacobsville. Between them, they've got six boys. Not a girl in either family."

At the mention of children, Grier became quiet. He and his houseguest, Tippy Moore, a rising movie star, had lost their baby just before Tippy's little brother was kidnapped and held for ransom. Tippy had traded herself for him, an act of courage that still made Grier proud. Their relationship was rocky even now, and Tippy was a potential victim of one of the kidnappers who'd eluded police in Manhattan.

Kemp glanced at him, aware of the older man's discomfort. "Sorry," he murmured. He knew about the baby because the story, a false and very unflattering one, had played out in the tabloids when Tippy had miscarried.

Grier let out a long breath. "I never knew I wanted kids," he said quietly, not meeting Kemp's gaze. "Hell of a way to find out I did."

"Life evens out," Kemp said philosophically. "You have bad days, then you have good ones to make up for them."

Grier's dark eyes twinkled. "I'm due about two years of good days."

Kemp laughed without humor. "Aren't we all?"

Grier's attention was captured by someone behind Kemp. He pursed his lips. "Your ex-secretary sure has changed."

Kemp was aware of his heart jumping at the statement. He turned his head and there was Violet. But she looked very different. She was wearing a neat little black skirt with a dropped-waist blue top that was cut modestly low in front. Her hair was around her shoulders, but it had frosted tips. She looked ten pounds lighter, and very pretty.

She noticed Kemp and her heart raced. Beside her Curt was watching the byplay with amusement, because Kemp couldn't seem to help staring any more than Violet could.

"I need to talk to someone," he told Violet. "Can you manage without me for a few minutes?"

"Yes!" She curbed her enthusiasm. "I mean, yes, that would be all right, Curt. Thanks."

He chuckled, winked at her, and strolled off.

Kemp walked up to her. He was dressed in an open-necked shirt with a sports coat and navy slacks. He looked expensive, sophisticated, and good enough to eat. Violet could hardly keep her eyes off him.

He was having a similar problem. It was odd how much Violet had been on his mind lately. He saw her in the office even when she wasn't there. He'd been uneasy since he'd seen her at her mother's house, and they'd parted on a harsh note.

"Still like working for Duke?" he queried stiffly.

She shrugged. "It's a job."

His eyebrow jerked. "Your hair looks nice," he murmured, reaching out to take a strand of it in his strong fingers. "I don't like frosting as a rule, but it suits you. You've lost more weight, too, haven't you?"

"It may look like it, but I haven't really," she replied, lost in a haze because of contact with him. "I've just been learning how to dress to make the most of what I have."

His eyes slid up to meet hers. "That's what life is all about, Violet," he said gently. "Learning how to make do with what we're given. You don't need to lose any more weight. You look great."

She flushed and smiled radiantly. "Do you…really think so?"

He moved a step closer, aware of pleasure centers opening all over his mind as he looked down at her. "Do you like trout?"

It was an odd question. She blinked. "Trout? Well, yes."

"Why don't you come over for lunch tomorrow? I'll fry trout and make a pasta salad to go with them. You can take some home to your mother."

Violet's jaw dropped. She stood gaping at him while she tried to decide, quickly, if she'd lost her mind and was having hallucinations.

Four

Her lack of response made Kemp uneasy and provoked a sarcastic response. He'd thought she'd jump at the chance. "What's the matter?" Kemp taunted. "Afraid to be alone with me outside the office?"

Violet gaped at him. "I am not...no...I don't think...I didn't say..." She cleared her throat. "I love trout. So does Mama."

His eyes twinkled. So he hadn't been wrong. She did still care about him. "So do I," he replied. "I panfry it in butter and spices. I have my own herb garden, even in the winter."

"It sounds delicious," she said breathlessly.

He still had the strand of her hair in his fingers. They became caressing, and his deep voice dropped even lower. "Do you like cats?"

She nodded.

"You may have a little trouble with Mee and Yow at first, but they'll get used to you."

Violet felt as if she'd stepped off a precipice and solved

the mystery of free flight. She was ecstatic. "I think cats are beautiful."

"Mine are Siamese. They're unique."

She smiled slowly. "I'll enjoy meeting them."

He let go of her hair and touched her soft cheek with his fingertips. They seemed to tingle at the contact. "About one in the afternoon tomorrow suit you?"

She nodded, speechless.

"Know how to get to my house?"

"Oh, yes," she said, and could have bitten her tongue for sounding so enthusiastic.

Kemp was eating it up. He knew it was a bad idea, encouraging her. At some point he was going to have to back away from her. He didn't want commitment. Not yet. But Violet was soft to the touch and lovely to look at. He'd been without a woman in his life for a long time. He was lonely. Surely it wouldn't hurt to have the occasional meal with her. Of course it wouldn't. He was enjoying her rapt expression. She made him feel as if he could conquer the world. For once in his life he was going to jump in with both feet without counting the cost.

"Then I'll expect you," he added.

She smiled up at him, her blue eyes wide and soft and hungry. "I'll look forward to it," she said huskily.

"So will I," he replied, and the smile faded for an instant as he searched her eyes for so long that she flushed and her breath rustled wildly in her throat.

"Kemp! Glad you could make it!" Tall, handsome Calhoun Ballenger moved forward to shake Kemp's hand and greet Violet. "Kemp, there's someone I'd like to introduce you to. Violet, you don't mind?"

"No, not at all," she lied.

"Tomorrow, at one," Kemp added before he walked away with Calhoun.

"Tomorrow," she replied.

* * *

Curt had to ask her twice if she was ready to leave. She hadn't had the opportunity to talk to Kemp any further, and he'd been called away suddenly to meet with a man who'd just been arrested. Before he left, he'd looked back at Violet with pale blue eyes that absolutely smoldered. She was still tingling an hour after he'd gone.

"What?" she asked abruptly, facing Curt. She flushed when he grinned. "Sorry," she began.

"Oh, I'm not upset," he replied, chuckling. "I'm glad to see that your ex-boss finally realized what he was missing."

She flushed even more. "It's not like that."

"I'm a man, Violet," he reminded her as they walked out to his car after making their goodbyes to their host. "I know a smitten man when I see one. Kemp's got it bad."

"Do you really think so?" she asked hopefully.

"I think so. Just go slowly," he advised. "He's pretty much a loner and he doesn't play around."

"I knew that already."

He turned toward her, serious for once. "What I meant," he said softly, "is that he's more vulnerable than a man who plays the field. And everybody knows he's not a marrying man, at least not visibly. You just step carefully, okay?"

"I will. Thanks for the advice, Curt."

He shrugged. "Story of my life. I'm always someone's big brother."

She grinned. "One day some lucky girl will carry you off," she promised.

He smiled back. "I hope it's a few years coming. I'm no more ready to settle down than your friend Kemp is. At least he's got a profession. I'm still drifting."

"Libby said you wanted to open a feed store."

He nodded. "It's the dream of my life."

"I hope you get to do it, Curt. I mean that."

He opened the door for her. "So do I. You're a nice girl, Violet."

"You're a nice man."

He chuckled. "Well, I'm accommodating, at least. Calhoun had quite a crowd today," he added when he'd climbed in under the wheel of his and Libby's old pickup truck.

"A big one. And some big money, too. I think he just may beat Senator Merrill for the Democratic nomination."

"I wouldn't be a bit surprised myself."

Violet told her mother about Kemp's invitation, and Mrs. Hardy grinned from ear to ear. "And how long have I been telling you that Mr. Kemp had more interest in you than a boss in his secretary?" she asked.

"It's only to eat a trout," Violet replied.

"He can eat trout by himself," her mother said sagely. "It's also interesting that Mr. Kemp, who never advertises his political affiliations, suddenly turned up at a campaign meeting."

"He likes Mr. Ballenger."

Mrs. Hardy pursed her lips. "I think somebody told him you were going to the meeting with Curt Collins."

She gasped. "Really?"

"Sometimes a man doesn't appreciate what he's got until some other man wants it. Or he thinks another man wants it." Mrs. Hardy's eyes twinkled. "We'll see, won't we, dear?"

Violet colored prettily and suggested a television program.

She didn't sleep. All night long, she saw Blake Kemp's eyes drilling into her own, she heard his voice, felt the touch of his fingers on her face. She tried on everything in her closet the next morning before she finally decided on a nice ankle-length sky-blue knit jumper with a white blouse under it and her embroidered denim jacket over it. She left her hair long.

"You look fine," Mrs. Hardy said from her bed when Violet went in to say goodbye.

"Are you sure you feel all right?" Violet worried.

"I'm just going to have a lazy Sunday," the older woman replied, smiling. "I wouldn't lie to you."

"All right. But if you need me…"

"The phone's right here, darling." Mrs. Hardy indicated it on the bedside table. "Now go and have a good time. I won't expect my trout anytime soon, by the way, and I've already had my breakfast."

"I'll bring you back something nice," Violet promised.

"Drive carefully."

Violet kissed her. "Always!"

She stopped on the front porch and looked down at her black loafers, worn with knee-high hose. She grimaced, because one of them was scuffed. But, she reasoned, Kemp was going to be more interested in the rest of her than in her shoes. She straightened her purse's shoulder strap over her shoulder and walked resolutely to her old but reliable car.

Kemp was on the front porch of his house when she drove up. It was a Victorian, with gingerbread patterned woodwork and a real turret room. The whole thing was painted white, brilliant and new-looking, and there was a porch swing and rocking chairs on the long, wide front porch. There were bird feeders everywhere. In the flower gardens flanking the porch, seeds were sprouting and rosebushes were putting out buds.

Violet took her purse and locked the car involuntarily before she pocketed her car key and walked up the steps.

"You like birds!" she exclaimed.

He laughed. He was dressed casually, as she was, in khaki

slacks and a blue knit designer shirt darker than the shade of his eyes behind the metal rims of his glasses.

"Yes, I like birds. But so do Mee and Yow, so I have to make sure they're both inside before I fill the feeders," he said on a chuckle.

"I have bird feeders at our place, too," Violet replied shyly. "I especially like the little birds, like the wrens and titmice."

"I prefer cardinals and blue jays."

"They're still birds," Violet said on a laugh.

He felt as if his feet were off the floor as he looked at her. Smiles transformed her oval face, made it bright and radiant—almost beautiful.

"Do you hire a gardener, or do you work in the yard yourself?" she asked, enthusiastic about the mass of flowering shrubs around the front yard.

"I do it," he replied. "I need to unwind from time to time."

"Yes, gardening is good for stress," she admitted. "I go through a lot of it myself. But I plant vegetables in our little garden, and I can or freeze them for the winter." She stopped suddenly, embarrassed, because the garden was a necessity for Violet and her mother, who had to budget furiously just to make ends meet. She doubted seriously if Kemp had ever budgeted in his life.

"I don't grow vegetables," he confessed. "Unless you count catnip, for the cats, and some herbs. I enjoy cooking."

"Me, too," she said. "Mama can do it, but I don't like to let her. She favors cast iron cookware, and it's heavy."

"She shouldn't be lifting it," he agreed. "I hope you're hungry."

She smiled. "I didn't even eat breakfast."

He smiled back. "Come in, then. It's all ready."

He opened the front door and let her walk in. There was a long hall with an elephant umbrella stand and a coatrack, with rooms opening off it on either side.

"Down the hall, to the left," he directed as he closed the front door.

The hall was painted a pale blue, with a chair rail in a darker shade, and wallpaper up to the crown. There was a pale blue carpet as well.

"You're probably thinking that it's hard to keep clean," Kemp remarked as he followed behind her. "And you're right. I have a cleaning crew come in to steam it frequently."

"I love the color," she remarked. "It reminds me of the ocean."

He laughed out loud. "It's the color of Yow's eyes," he added. "And she knows it. She loves to sprawl on the carpet. Mee prefers the couch or my bed."

Violet caught her breath as she walked into the formal dining room. There was a cherry wood table, already set with linen and crystal and china, and beyond it was a kitchen that would have been any cook's dream. There was a tile floor, modern appliances, a huge combination sink, and a counter big enough to use for dressing half a steer. Over the sink was a large window overlooking the pasture and forest behind the house.

"I'll bet you enjoy working in here," she remarked.

"I do. I like enough space to move in. Cramped kitchens are the very devil."

"Indeed they are, and I could write you a book on them," Violet confessed. "I bump into the refrigerator or the stove every time I turn around at home."

"What would you like to drink?" he asked, opening the refrigerator. "I've got soft drinks, iced tea, or coffee."

"I love coffee, if it isn't too much trouble."

He grinned at her. "I always have a pot warming," he said.

He got down two china cups and saucers and poured coffee into them. "Cream and sugar on the table."

He carried them to the places, which were already set, amid platters of fish, vegetables, fresh rolls and even a cake.

"This looks wonderful!" she exclaimed.

"I counted on your being punctual," he said with a glance. "You always are."

He seated her, and then himself.

"I like to make a good impression," she told him.

He chuckled. "Help yourself."

She looked around curiously as she helped herself to trout and rolls and a potato casserole that smelled delicious. "Where are the cats?"

"They're shy around people they don't know," he said nonchalantly. "They'll show up when I cut the cake. They beg for cake."

"You're kidding!" she exclaimed.

He laughed. "I'm not. You'll see."

They spoke about the upcoming election and the local political gossip during the meal. Violet was impressed with his culinary skills. He was an accomplished cook.

"Have you always been able to knock out a meal?" she wondered aloud.

"I was in the Army—special forces," he replied simply. "I had to learn how to cook."

"You were in Cag Hart's division, weren't you?"

He nodded. "So was Matt Caldwell. A lot of local guys turned up there."

She didn't know how far to push her luck. Someone had told her that he didn't like to talk about his unit's participation in the earlier Iraq conflict. But he got up to slice cake and two Siamese voices grew louder.

"See?" he asked, when the cats appeared on either side of him, their faces lifted as they meowed, sounding for all the world like little children.

"They have unique voices, don't they?" she asked, fascinated.

"They do. And Siamese have one other peculiarity—they

can reach completely behind their heads. They have claws and they aren't shy about using them," he added with a warning glance. "Go slowly, and everything will be all right."

"Do you give them cake?" she asked.

He laughed. "Tiny little bites," he said, confessing. "I don't want to make them fat…"

Violet flushed red.

He ground his teeth and looked at her soulfully. "I didn't mean that the way you're taking it, Violet," he said gently. "I don't think you're fat. You look exactly as a woman should look, in every way."

"You said…" she began.

"I took a bad day out on you," he replied, "and I'm sorrier than you know. It was a vicious thing to do. I made you quit, and I never meant to."

For an apology, it was wholesale and flattering. She looked at him without blinking. "Really?"

He relaxed when he saw the combined pleasure and fascination in her face. She made him tingle just by looking at him. He wanted to drag her out of her chair and kiss the breath from her body. The thought shocked him. He stood with the knife poised over the cake, just staring at her.

The flush grew. She felt her heart racing like mad in her chest. Her lips parted as she tried to breathe normally.

"A lot of it was the way you dressed," he said tautly when he managed to drag his eyes back to the cake. "I like the new wardrobe. It fits properly. Baggy dresses and blouses aren't flattering for a full-figured woman."

She didn't take offense. He was looking at her as if he wanted, very badly, to kiss her. As he slid a piece of cake onto a saucer and put it in front of her, she looked up into his pale eyes with pure lust.

It had been a long time between women, but Kemp hadn't forgotten the way a woman looked when she wanted to be kissed. Absently, his lean hand went to the back of Violet's chair and he bent toward her confidently.

Her intake of breath made him hesitate, but only for a second. His other hand came up to her softly rounded chin and he tilted it up, just a fraction. "Don't make such heavy weather of it," he whispered as his mouth hovered over hers. "I want to kiss you as you much as you want me to."

"Re…really?" she choked.

He smiled gently. "Really."

His lips teased over her full mouth, nibbling her upper lip while he tasted it with a lazy stroke of his tongue. Violet jumped and shivered. The contact was completely out of her experience. She'd dated a few boys, but she didn't seem to appeal to any of them physically. This was different. She wished she knew what to do, so that he wouldn't stop.

He lifted his head and looked into her rapt, expectant eyes. She was breathing like a distance runner. Her breasts were shaking under the whip of her pulse. He'd thought she was at least a little experienced, but it seemed he was wrong.

His thumb moved to her lower lip and tugged it down gently as his head bent again.

"We have to start somewhere," he breathed as his mouth opened against her full, soft lips.

Violet shivered. Her hands went to his arms, her fingers digging in. He was muscular. He didn't look muscular in his suits, but she could feel the strength at this range. She moaned, a whisper of sound that drew his head up.

His eyes met hers, and there was no teasing in them now. They were intent, darker, hungry.

Her fingers lifted to his cheek, hesitantly. "Don't…stop," she pleaded in a soft, shaky whisper.

A muscle in his jaw tensed. He bent again, his own heart racing. "Violet," he whispered.

This time the kiss wasn't teasing, tender, or brief. He

ground his mouth into her soft lips. She moaned again, and this time her hands met behind his neck and dug in. His mouth grew demanding.

There was another moan, but this one wasn't passionate.

His head jerked back. Violet reached down and grabbed her ankle just as Yow drew back, hissing.

"Yow!" Kemp exclaimed, moving around the chair to shoo the cat away while he knelt and examined Violet's ankle. It was bleeding. "I'm sorry! I wouldn't have had this happen for the world!"

"I must have stepped on her tail, poor thing," Violet faltered. It was exciting to kiss Blake Kemp. It was equally exciting to have him at her feet, concerned for her.

"You were kissing me," he corrected. "They're jealous of any attention I pay to other people."

"This has…happened before?" she asked miserably.

"Yes. Well, no, not like this," he said. "Mee sank her teeth into Cy Parks one day when he was having coffee with me in the kitchen."

"I see," she began.

He gave her a wicked grin. "I wasn't kissing him."

She burst out laughing.

He stood up, pulling back her chair. He tugged her to her feet and suddenly swung her up into his arms. She gasped and clutched at his shoulders.

He raised an eyebrow rakishly. "Now it's my ankles that will be in danger. I have to clean that and put antiseptic ointment on it," he mused as he turned and carried her down the hall toward the bedrooms.

"I'm too heavy!" she protested.

"You're not," he assured her. He looked down at her in his arms. He felt several inches taller. She was delightful close up. He enjoyed kissing her. He'd liked to have done it again, but this wasn't the time.

He put her down on the vanity in the huge, blue-patterned tile bathroom. There was a whirlpool bath and an enormous space that held commode, vanity, chair, and a linen closet, as well as a large medicine chest.

He fumbled in the chest for what he needed, tugged a washcloth out of a drawer and proceeded to clean and bandage the wound.

Yow peered into the bathroom, her blue eyes huge in her triangle-shaped face.

"No tuna for you tonight, young lady," Blake told her firmly.

She flattened her ears and hissed at Violet.

"And none tomorrow, either," he added curtly.

Yow turned her back and flounced out. Mee, in a conciliatory tone, meowed at the door and walked in, watching the byplay curiously but without much antagonism.

"Beautiful girl," Violet mused, lowering her fingers for the cat to sniff.

Mee sniffed them, rubbed her face against them, and then wrapped her lean body around Violet's legs.

"You can have tuna," Blake told the cat.

The purring grew louder.

Violet stroked the cat, but her eyes and her heart were on Blake's bent head as he put a sticky bandage over the scratch.

"It should be fine," he said.

"Of course it will be," she assured him, smiling down as he finished. "Thanks."

"I'm really sorry," he said again as he gathered up the first aid supplies and put them away. "Yow's spoiled."

"I love cats," Violet said, still stroking Mee. "I'd have loved to have some, if Mama wasn't allergic."

"I don't know what I'd do without mine. Although there are times when I'm tempted to try," he added, with a glowering look toward the door where Yow had reappeared and was hissing again.

"You live alone," she said. "It's natural that they'd resent strangers."

He bent down and drew her gently to her feet. "You're no stranger," he said huskily as his eyes searched hers. "I don't think you ever were."

She felt such elation that she could hardly get her breath. Just weeks ago they'd been mortal enemies. Then, suddenly, they were almost intimate. It was a shock. It was…wonderful.

"Your eyes can't hide anything," he murmured, bending toward her.

She glanced worriedly at her ankles, and he laughed.

He picked her up again, shifting her in his arms. "Feel safer?" he murmured, staring at her mouth.

"Much," she agreed, and her arms tightened boldly around his neck.

With a long sigh, he bent his head and kissed her, very tenderly. His teeth nibbled at her lower lip until her mouth opened. He took immediate advantage of the opportunity, and she felt her whole body go hot as he dragged her closer, so that her full breasts rubbed against his muscular chest.

He groaned, and the kiss grew hotter, longer, more passionate. His arms contracted hungrily.

She gave him back the kiss with more enthusiasm than expertise, but he didn't seem to mind. She sighed under the hard crush of his mouth and sank into dreams. It was sweeter than she'd ever dared hope it might be.

She felt as if her whole body was shattering with pleasure.

Blake's head lifted. He turned it, listening. That hadn't been her imagination. Something really had shattered. "Yow!" he growled.

He put Violet down and rushed back down the hall ahead of her. He made it into the dining room just in time to see Yow feasting on Violet's piece of cake, on the floor, in the ruins of the saucer it had been placed in.

"Yow!" he bit off.

The cat jumped back and hissed at Violet. For good measure she hissed at Blake, too, and ran quickly out of the room.

Mee, seeing an opening, rubbed against Blake's legs while she eyed the cake on the floor.

Blake picked up the saucer pieces. While he was putting them into the trash, Mee grabbed up a piece of cake and trotted into the kitchen with it.

"That cat," he was muttering.

Violet was chuckling, happier than she'd been in years, despite the cat's antagonism. It was a rare look at Blake's private life, at the man he was when he wasn't working. She liked what she saw. His affection for the cats was obvious, even through his frustration with Yow.

"They're very different, aren't they?" she asked while he took the lion's share of the cake away from a frustrated Mee and put it in the trash, too.

"They're maddening from time to time," he admitted. "But I suppose they'd taste terrible, even if I do have infrequent visions of serving them up in a casserole."

"You wouldn't dare!" she exclaimed, laughing.

He shrugged. "Well, not sober," he confessed.

She grinned at him, her whole face radiant with the sudden, new relationship that was building between them.

She looked so pretty that Blake stopped what he was doing and just stared at her. Why hadn't he realized how pretty she was? he wondered.

Violet saw the look and was mesmerized by it. She stood staring back at him, while time stood still around them.

Five

Violet folded her hands in front of her, self-consciously. "I really like your house," she said, for something to break the silence.

He smiled. "I'm glad."

"I like the cats, too. In spite of everything," she added. "It's only a scratch."

He glowered toward the doorway, where Yow was looking in again. Mee was still twirling around Violet's ankles. "We'll have to work on Yow's social skills. Maybe she lacks proper company. I might buy her a dog."

"You wouldn't!" Violet exclaimed, laughing.

He gave her a wicked look. "A big, ugly dog with a bad attitude," he added.

"You'd turn up in court as a defendant."

"Not unless Yow can afford legal representation," he assured her.

She laughed. It was amazing how carefree she felt with

him, a man who'd intimidated her from their very first meeting when she'd worked for him. He was another man entirely
away from the office.

"Well, there's still cake," he pointed out. "We'd better get
it while we can, before Yow tries again."

"What kind is it?" she asked as she seated herself at the
table again.

"Pound cake. It's the only cake I can do myself."

"My favorite kind, too. I can make a layer cake, but I like
these better."

He put a slice on a plate, and a fork, in front of her. "More
coffee?"

"Please," she replied.

He poured more coffee and they settled down with their
cake, but she noticed that Blake kept a careful eye on the
doorway in case Yow made another appearance.

He wouldn't let her help with the dishes, insisting that he
could do them later. Instead, he walked her out onto the
porch and settled her beside him in the porch swing.

"I love this," she said. "We used to have a porch swing,
before we lost everything," she mused. "I loved sitting in it,
especially in the spring and summer. We had a big yard with
pecan trees and a mesquite tree, and Mama had a flower garden, very much like yours."

He slid his arm behind her head and curled his long fingers comfortably into her hair. "It must be hard for both of
you."

"We're getting by," she said softly. "I don't really mind.
I'm just sorry about Daddy, and how he died." She looked
up at him. "You haven't heard anything about the autopsy
yet?"

"Maybe next week," he replied. "I'll tell you the minute
I know for sure. Then we'll both break it to your mother."

"That's very kind of you," she said.

He bent and touched his lips to her forehead. "I'm a kind man," he murmured, laughing softly. "I don't even kick cats when they deserve it."

She smiled back, leaning closer. She loved being near him, feeling his breath on her face, his fingers in her hair.

Blake was amazed at how receptive she was to his advances, how hungrily she met them. He hadn't analyzed his feelings for Violet. He wasn't going to. Not yet. But she kindled fires in his blood that he hadn't felt since Shannon Culbertson's death.

Shannon. His eyes grew dark and quiet as he stared over Violet's head and memories flooded in on him. He'd loved her. He'd given his heart completely, recklessly, without any thought for the future. Shannon had died, and his life had shattered overnight. He remembered that headlong passion with faint apprehension. It was dangerous to love. Very dangerous.

Violet didn't know what he was thinking, but she felt a sudden remoteness from him. She noticed that he was staring into space, thinking. Perhaps he was having second thoughts about the direction their relationship was taking. Was he sorry that he'd kissed her?

He felt her intent stare. He turned his head and looked down into her eyes, searching them slowly. The look was more intimate than a kiss. His body began to swell from the intensity of it.

"Is something wrong?" she asked after a minute.

His fingers touched her chin, drawing it up. "I have cold feet."

"I don't understand."

He drew in a long breath. "It's too quick, Violet," he murmured, looking at her. "I'm not sure I'm ready for this."

"For feeding me trout?" she asked, wide-eyed.

He shook his head. "No. For…this."

He bent and kissed her, very gently. He lifted his head. "I like kissing you."

She smiled slowly. "I like kissing you, too."

"To what end?"

She blinked. "Excuse me?"

"I don't want to get married," he said bluntly.

She felt all at sea, confused and uncertain.

He stared down into her wide eyes. She looked miserable and he felt confused. "Forget it," he murmured, dropping his stare to her soft eyes. "I'm just talking. I don't even know what I'm talking about."

"I know about her," she blurted out.

He scowled. "Her?"

"Shannon Culbertson," she said, averting her gaze to the budding rosebushes. "I'm sorry it happened like that. It must have been devastating for you."

He couldn't think of another single person he wouldn't have cursed for mentioning her name. But it didn't feel at all uncomfortable to discuss Shannon with Violet. She had a tender heart. He ached for comfort. He'd never had it.

"She was beautiful," he replied. "Young and full of fun and promise. I loved her until she was an obsession. I didn't think I could go on living when she died."

"But you did," she replied. "You're stronger than you realize."

"You have an odd effect on me," he murmured.

"What sort?" she asked, studying him.

One shoulder lifted and fell. His eyes went back to the landscape as he rocked the swing lazily into motion. "I don't talk about her. I haven't in years."

She sighed and rested her head on his shoulder, staring across his broad chest toward the distant highway. "You can't bury the past," she said absently. "It affects everything we do, everything we are."

He frowned. "Did you lose someone?"

She laughed. "Me? When I was in high school, I weighed even more than I do now. My parents sent me to a private school because they thought I might not get picked on as much. But I did. There are always the beautiful people who feel privileged to comment on the less fortunate. I hated school."

"I thought schools were cracking down on bullies."

"If they crack down very hard, they tend to get sued," she pointed out, with a speaking look in his direction.

He chuckled. "I don't take frivolous lawsuits," he reminded her.

"Plenty of other lawyers do. Then they get huge awards, which they keep the lion's share of. Then insurance, and everything else goes sky high."

He scowled. "Well, you have got a point."

"I make up in intelligence for what I lack in looks," she murmured.

He tilted her face up to his and searched her blue, blue eyes. "Violet," he said softly, "there's nothing wrong with the way you look. I had a bad morning and I took it out on you that day. I've been trying to find a way to apologize every since. You look like a woman should."

She studied him with big, curious eyes. He was very handsome. She was fascinated by the way he was looking at her, as if he really did find her enchanting. She smiled slowly.

"Ahh," he cautioned in a husky tone. "Looking at me like that will get you into trouble."

"It will?" she asked hopefully.

The humor went right by him. His eyes had dropped to her full, soft mouth and he was feeling a surge of hunger. Some tiny voice was urging caution. He ignored it and pulled Violet closer. His hard mouth curved down against her soft one, teasing lightly until she relaxed and leaned against his chest. His long fingers slid into her thick, soft hair, and tugged her head farther back on his broad shoulder.

His fingers were at her nape, teasing, tracing, while his mouth slowly penetrated the tight line of her lips.

She stiffened, but he persisted. When she still wouldn't give him what he wanted, his lean hand slid right over her full breast and contracted gently with the nipple trapped between his thumb and his hand. She gasped and shivered, giving him access to the dark inner softness of her mouth. She felt his tongue slide sensuously inside and a curious swelling sensation overtook her body.

His hand became insistent on her breast, searching for buttons. He made an opening and his fingers slid inside it, right onto the warm silkiness of her bare skin. She moaned huskily. Her arms reached up and enclosed his neck while she gave in to the unreality of being in his arms, being desired by him.

The kiss became passionate, demanding. She moaned again. Vaguely, she felt him pulling her up. He bent and lifted her, his mouth still enclosing her yielded, hungry lips. He carried her into the house, kicking the door shut behind him.

He started toward the bedroom, but his body was in agony. Too many years of abstinence had left him powerless with Violet's mouth promising heaven. He made it to the living room and slid her onto the sofa, but there wasn't really room for both of them on it. She was as hungry as he was, and their restless movements landed them on the carpet between the sofa and the coffee table.

He started to lift his head, but she pulled his mouth back over hers. The sensations were like waves of pleasure that rocked her in his hard arms, and she didn't want them to stop. She didn't want him to stop. She'd never felt such physical delight in all her life, and she wasn't willing to give it up just yet.

Blake was feeling something similar. It had been a long time since he'd had such a willing, hungry partner. Even Shannon, although she loved him, had been receptive but not eager when he made love to her. Violet was different. She tasted of honey. He loved the feel of her mouth under his. He loved the feverish response of her body to his lightest touch. He loved the soft little noises she made, the tiny gasps that pulsed rhythmically out of her throat as his caresses became quickly more intimate.

She felt cool air on her breasts and opened her eyes just a breath. Her clothes were open all the way down the front, and her bra was unhooked. His eyes were a darkened, passionate blue as they caressed her bare breasts, feeding on their ample curves and the taut mauve rise of her nipples. He bent, his mouth opening as he eased down beside her again and took her into his mouth.

She arched completely off the floor, sobbing. "Yes," she choked. "Yes!"

What little control he'd had left was gone at once. She was as hungry as he was. He didn't think about afterward. He was too far gone to care about tomorrow. There was only the painful need that stretched his powerful body like rope over her rippling, soft body. Years of abstinence took control of his will.

His hands were deft and efficient. Within seconds, the barriers were all gone, and his mouth was moving hungrily over Violet's soft belly, down to the inside of her thighs.

While he kissed her, he touched her, in ways and places she'd only read about. She hadn't dreamed that the sensations would be so overwhelming. When the first ripples of ecstasy worked their way down her aching body, she was far beyond any sort of protest. She loved him. He wanted her. She was becoming a woman, truly a woman, for the first time. She wanted nothing more than to go on being kissed and touched and caressed to madness in his arms.

Somehow, it never occurred to her that the first time might be uncomfortable; or that he might not know it was her first time. Most women were experienced by the time they reached Violet's age. But Violet was a late bloomer.

She felt the sudden penetration with a hungry delight that turned quite suddenly to discomfort, and then pain. She stiffened and gasped, her nails digging into his back.

Shivering with desire, he managed to lift his head and look into her wide, shocked eyes.

He felt the barrier. Why hadn't he realized how difficult this might be? Because he was out of his mind with desire, that was why. And he couldn't stop. He couldn't...!

His knee pressed her legs wide apart, despite her silent protests, and his hand went quickly between them. He watched her face the whole time, watched fear and pain slowly give way to sharp pleasure.

Her nails bit into his back again, but not in pain this time. She was shuddering rhythmically with every sharp, deep downward movement of his hips. Her legs widened without any more coaxing. Her hips arched up to meet his. And still he held her eyes, watching her as he took her.

It was the most erotic experience of his entire life. Despite his experience, and he had some, it was new territory for him. He had inhibitions as surely as Violet had. Most of his encounters had been in dark rooms, at night. It was the first time he'd gone this far in broad daylight, and that was as erotic as the sight of Violet's pink nudity under him on the carpet. He began to shiver with each rough movement as he found his way ever deeper into her soft body.

"I've never done this...in broad daylight. And I've never watched, Violet," he bit off, his deep voice strained as he looked into her blue eyes.

She swallowed, hard. Her lips were parted on gasping breaths as the pleasure built and began to funnel up in her.

She stared into his eyes, shivering, climbing some invisible ladder of pleasure toward what felt like an unbearable goal.

"I've...never," she choked.

His jaw clenched as the pleasure began to bite into him. "I know," he groaned harshly. His eyes closed on a wave of ecstasy that arched him above her, his hips pinning hers violently as he drove for fulfillment. "God...I can't...stop!" he moaned.

Violet's knees drew up on either side of him, enhancing the madness of delight. She arched again and again, her eyes wide, her mouth wide, as she looked into his eyes. They were almost black with desire.

"I feel you," she whispered brokenly. "I feel you...in me!"

The anguish tripled at the erotic little whisper. His body ground hers into the carpet with violent, urgent motions that were more desperate than experienced. Her back was going to be raw, he thought in one last burst of sanity. Then he felt her convulse under him and cry out, and contract around him. He exploded, his eyes closed, his body helplessly impaling her in one last furious downward movement that lifted him to a level of climax he'd never known.

Violet felt him, tasted him, bonded with him in that space of seconds. The pleasure slowly fell to bearable levels and she wanted to weep, because it was so exquisite, and so very brief. She looked at him while he gave in to his own need, her eyes hungry on the length of his body, rippling muscle and thick hair on his chest, down to the flat stomach that was pressed so close to hers, to the long, powerful legs lying between her white thighs.

It should have been embarrassing, to see them like that. But she was only fascinated by the newness of intimacy.

She looked back up to see his face clenched, damp with sweat, as he slowly came back to himself. His eyes opened, dark, somber, sated.

She reached up and touched his mouth. She felt his body shivering in the aftermath, as hers was. He looked…shattered.

He collapsed on her, his forearms catching most of his formidable weight. His face pulsed at her throat, damp and sucking at breath. He shuddered. Her arms slid around him, cradling him. She felt him against every inch of her. She felt him, still inside her, still pulsing softly.

"Gosh," she whispered, awed. Her legs curved around the back of his and her body lifted in soft entreaty.

"Optimist," he murmured.

She laughed softly. She knew what he meant. Men spent themselves, and then it took a long time before they were capable again. She'd never indulged, but she'd heard other women talk.

"When I felt you stiffen, I could have shot myself," he said at her ear. "I lost it. I knew you were a virgin, and I still couldn't stop."

Her hands smoothed his dark, wavy hair. She looked up at the ceiling, vaguely aware of the cats moving around the room, of a breeze fluttering the curtains, of a distant car passing on the highway on the horizon. She'd never been so close to another human being. She knew, finally, what it was to be a woman. She'd never dreamed that it would be Blake who taught her how to make love.

He drew in a long breath and rolled over onto his back, bringing her over him so that he could look up into her wide blue eyes.

His hand went between them and came up with a faint trace of blood.

She blushed.

He searched her eyes for a long time. "I didn't have the presence of mind to think about protection, either."

She didn't know what to say. She was still halfway in and halfway out of a new reality.

His hands slid down her body to her wide, soft hips. "Lift up," he murmured sensuously.

She did, curious, until she saw his eyes go hungrily to her breasts. His hands slid up to them, cupping them softly. He eased her onto her back and his mouth made a meal of them, kissing and tasting until she rippled all over with renewed desire.

He groaned as his body responded with renewed arousal and sudden urgency. "Are you sore?" he asked roughly.

"I…well, I don't…ouch!" she gasped when he touched her where the tissues were torn from their first intimacy.

He ground his teeth together. "Sorry," he whispered.

She could feel how hungry he was. "You can," she whispered back. "It's okay."

He felt those words to the soles of his feet. She would have let him, despite the pain. It humbled him to know that.

He bent to her mouth and kissed her softly, with exquisite tenderness. She tugged at his hips, but he didn't respond.

"No," he said softly, and he smiled at her. "Not unless you can take as much pleasure from my body as I take from yours."

She was fascinated by the reply.

He kissed her again, very softly, and then rolled away from her. He tugged his clothes back on and stood up to finish the fastenings. He looked down at her as she pulled her discarded dress against her breasts and stared at him confusedly.

"I'll make some coffee," he said quietly, aware of her sudden embarrassment. "Then we'll talk."

He walked away. She struggled quickly back into her things, noting the curious stares of the twin Siamese cats, who probably had never seen such confusing behavior from their resident human pet. It made her self-conscious.

By the time he came back with a tray, she was sitting on the couch feeling waves of embarrassment and shame.

He sat down beside her, fixed a cup of coffee the way he knew she liked it, and handed it to her. He saw the tears she was trying not to shed.

He reached over for a tissue from the box he kept by the lamp and wiped her eyes with a tenderness that said more than words.

"I haven't had a woman for over two years," he said bluntly. "I'm sorry. I lost control the minute I started kissing you."

"It's all right," she choked, sipping coffee. "I didn't exactly fight for my honor." Tears started rolling again, staining her cheeks while she tried not to let him see how upset she was.

He took the coffee away from her, tugged her into his arms, and dragged her over into his lap. He held her while she cried, rocking her in the silence of the room. He felt satiated. His body was more relaxed than it had been in years. He felt young, vital, full of fire. He smiled at the difference a few torrid minutes had made in their tumultuous relationship.

"I'm sorry," she choked. "I'm acting like a child."

He kissed her wet eyelids. "First times are traumatic," he murmured, drying her eyes again with the tissue.

"Was yours?" she asked, curious.

He laughed. "The first time I tried to have sex, I was seventeen. I was dating an older girl and we were in the back seat of my parents' car at a country drive-in, one of the last few in Texas," he recalled. "We were going at it hot and heavy when my zipper stuck."

She stared at him, fascinated.

He laughed again. "I couldn't get it to budge. I couldn't get my jeans off with it zipped. And if I broke the zipper, I'd never have gotten past my mother to my room." He shook his head. "She was experienced, and furious. She called me a clumsy fool and said she couldn't imagine why girls went

out with me. I took her home and never phoned her again.
She didn't know it was my first time, which was all that
saved my pride."

"I can't imagine you being clumsy," she said, fascinated
by him.

He kissed the tip of her nose. "We all start somewhere,"
he mused lazily. He traced around her soft mouth. "But you
were my first virgin," he whispered, holding her eyes.

Her lips parted. "I was?"

He nodded. He pushed back her disheveled hair. "I wasn't
sure I knew enough to spare you the pain."

"You did, though," she whispered, and averted her eyes,
flushing.

He'd noticed. He felt ten feet tall. He knew that she'd cli-
maxed, and not just the one time. He'd given her fulfillment,
despite the rough beginning. It made him proud.

He cradled her close, wrapping her up in his arms with her
face in his warm throat. He rocked her hungrily, his body still
tingling with remembered pleasure. "I'd forgotten how it
felt," he whispered. "I suppose I've been half-alive, without
knowing it."

"So have I," she replied drowsily. She curled closer into
his powerful body.

He kissed her hair. "I'm sorry I made you sore," he whispered. "It was unavoidable."

"I know."

He sat holding her for a long time, so contented that he
didn't realize how late it was getting until the automatic
lights outside began to come on.

"Goodness," she exclaimed when she noticed, sitting up
on his lap. "I have to get home. Mama will be worried." She
stopped, aghast when she remembered her mother and her
responsibilities. She remembered what she'd done with
Kemp and she felt self-conscious and uncomfortable.

He knew that. He could see it in her expression. He didn't know what to say to make things right.

"If anything happens, we'll handle it," he said softly. "Don't beat yourself to death worrying. Okay?"

We'll handle it. Did he mean he'd pay for a termination? She felt sick at her stomach. What in the world had she been thinking? She'd just had sex with her former boss and he wasn't a marrying man. He wasn't going to start hearing violins if she turned up pregnant. He was going to suggest a practical solution. But she wasn't going to be able to agree with that. It just wasn't possible.

"I can see the thoughts in your mind, Violet," he said abruptly. "Let's not face problems before they appear."

She swallowed. "You're right, of course." She got to her feet unsteadily, and looked around as if she didn't quite know where she was.

Kemp got up, too. "Do you want me to follow you home, just in case?" he asked.

She looked up. "In case of what?"

"You don't drive at night much," he said. He scowled. "There are drunks on the roads at night around here."

"I won't have any trouble," she assured him.

"Except when it comes to living with what just happened," he remarked.

She picked up her purse and sweater and turned to look at him. "What?"

He shoved his hands into his pockets. "You're a Puritan, Violet," he said somberly. "You weren't a virgin by accident."

She colored. "I don't date much…"

He waved away the rest of the reply. "You're in love with me. I've always known it. There isn't any other reason that would make you give yourself to a man without marriage."

She glared at him. She hated being so transparent.

He moved closer, taking her gently by the shoulders.

"You'll work for me until we find out, one way or another, if there are going to be any consequences."

"I should never have…!"

He kissed her mouth closed. "We're both human." He searched her eyes. "I love the way you were with me," he added huskily. "It was the most exciting encounter of my life, Violet. I think I could live on it, if I had to. You were…extraordinary."

"I didn't know anything," she blurted out.

"Instinct must go a long way, then." He bent and kissed her again. "Try not to be ashamed of something so beautiful," he added quietly. "We have a lot in common. I think we'll find even more, as we go along."

He was saying something incredible. She stared up at him, fascinated.

"I was happy being alone until you came along and shook up my life," he murmured absently, watching her closely. "I can't go back."

"You can't?"

He brought her soft palm to his mouth and kissed it hungrily. "In a few days, I think we might go and look at rings," he said hesitantly, and his high cheekbones took on a ruddy color.

"Rings?"

His thumb rubbed over her ring finger. "Rings."

She couldn't manage a single word.

His blue eyes were somber. "Today was a beginning. Not the end."

Her lips parted as she studied him, with love radiating from her face. He saw it, and felt humbled by it. He'd never been with a woman who was so violently in love with him. He felt cosseted, valued, possessed.

He drew her against him, aware that he became aroused the instant he felt her soft breasts against his chest. That hadn't happened even with Shannon, when he was much younger. Violet lit fires in his body.

"Feel that?" he whispered as he bent to her mouth. "You arouse me so much that it hurts."

She opened her mouth when she felt his lips on it. He built the kiss, lifting her free of the floor in his embrace. "I would still let you," she whispered.

"I know," he whispered back. "You're part of me now. I'm part of you. Kiss me…"

The kiss was long, hard, passionate. When he finally put her down, she was trembling.

"Go home," he said firmly, leading her to the door with her purse in his hand.

"Throwing me out?" she teased.

He chuckled. "Saving you," he murmured wickedly. "I need a cold shower."

She touched his chest with her hand, dizzy and aching with new sensations, new joy. "I know you already know it," she said softly. "But I love you."

He traced her mouth with his fingertip. The words bit into him, made him feel guilty. He wanted her, but he didn't feel that emotion for her. Not yet. He just smiled. "Drive carefully. Call me when you get home."

He didn't say it, but he had to feel something powerful for her, she was certain of it. She beamed. "Okay. Good night."

"Good night, angel," he said softly.

He watched her walk away with feelings of utter self-contempt. He'd taken advantage of what she felt for him, lost control and put her at risk. Now he had to stand by and wait to find out if she became pregnant, knowing that if she did, he'd be forced to marry her to save her reputation. It wasn't the best night of his life, despite the lingering pleasure that reminded him of the afternoon.

Six

Violet managed to slip into her house without being seen by her mother. She was disheveled and her hair was a mess. Her mother wasn't blind or stupid, she'd know that something torrid had been going on. To prevent any uncomfortable questions, Violet had called to her and then went straight to her room without letting herself be seen.

From there, she went to the kitchen, trying not to let her mind wander to the afternoon. Then she remembered that she'd promised to bring her mother some trout. She groaned inwardly. She heated her mother a bowl of soup and crackers for supper.

"I'm sorry about the trout," she began. But she was beaming and she couldn't help it.

Mrs. Hardy grinned. "Never mind that. Soup is fine. You've got feathers on your lips, my darling cat," she chided. "So what's going on with you and that dishy man?"

So much for deterring her mother's suspicions. Violet

blushed, grinning back. "The boss man is talking about rings."

Her mother gasped. "Darling!"

Violet laughed. "Can you believe it? And we were fighting and giving each other fits just last week!"

"He didn't really know you before, though," the older woman pointed out as she sipped soup from a spoon. "You were too shy to be yourself with him."

"I was," Violet agreed, vaguely ashamed of what had happened, just the same.

"Did he mention a date?"

Violet shook her head. "We're going to take it one day at a time," she replied.

Mrs. Hardy only smiled. She knew that when couples got to the ring stage, weddings very often came quickly. "I've only ever wanted to live long enough to see you married and secure," she said absently.

"You'd better be around longer than that," Violet chided. "I can't do without you!"

"Bosh," the other woman murmured. "You've got your own life to live. I'm just about done with mine."

"Don't you talk like that," her daughter chided. "You're not nearly done. You have so much to look forward to!"

"Such as?" Mrs. Hardy asked, her eyes lackluster.

"Grandchildren!" she replied, and blushed again, because she could already be pregnant.

The older woman sat very still. "Grandchildren. Why…I hadn't thought…" She glanced at Violet. "Does he want children, then?"

"Of course," Violet said, smiling.

"He must have changed his mind," Mrs. Hardy mused to herself.

Violet felt a sinking sensation. "What do you mean?"

"Oh, it's just something he mentioned that day he came

over to talk to me, dear," she said, sipping more soup. "He said that he'd never have a child."

Violet felt sick. "Did he?"

Her mother hadn't noticed Violet's sudden lack of color and enthusiasm. She was thinking. "Men often think like that, until they have a child. But he was rather emphatic about it, just the same."

"I wonder why," Violet murmured aloud, uncomfortable.

Her mother glanced at her worriedly. "You mustn't let on that I told you," she said.

"Told me what, Mother?"

Mrs. Hardy grimaced. "Mr. Kemp is a very upright man these days, but he was young and irresponsible once. I'd heard something about the Culbertson girl, from a nurse I know. I asked him about it. He was shocked enough to tell me the truth about her. She was pregnant when she died. It was his child. He hadn't known about it, although he would have married her sooner if he had. The coroner covered up her pregnancy, to spare her parents the embarrassment. But it affected him terribly. He lost not only his fiancée, but his child as well. He said that just the thought of a child gave him nightmares now, brought it all back to haunt him."

Violet sat down, hard. It was worse than she'd imagined. Blake didn't want children. She'd pushed him off balance and they'd had unprotected sex. He was making the best of things, but he'd never said that he loved her and he'd intimated that if she turned up pregnant, they'd have to make arrangements. Could that mean that he didn't want a child, ever, after what had happened with his fiancée?

She felt sick to her soul. What was she going to do?

"Dear, what's wrong?" Mrs. Hardy asked with a frown.

Violet forced a smile. "Nothing. I shouldn't be jealous of a dead woman, should I?" she added, leading her mother right into the false conclusion that she was thinking about Shannon.

Mrs. Hardy relaxed. "Yes, dear. You shouldn't."

Violet changed the subject. But she didn't sleep very much that night. She was sick with worry. How could she have been so blind and stupid? She was going to pay a high price for her one hour of passion. She'd thought it was worth anything at the time. Now, she wasn't so sure.

She went to work Monday morning with uncertain feelings. She dreaded and anticipated seeing Blake again, both at once. Duke Wright smiled at her as he put her to work on new herd records, and he looked as if he might have known something about her day at Blake Kemp's house. But he didn't say anything.

Curt did. He grinned at her as he paused beside her desk. "I hear you were out at Kemp's place over the weekend," he murmured.

She gasped. "How…?"

"Jacobsville is a small town," he said pleasantly. "Kemp's driveway faces a major highway. Your car would stick out in a parking lot."

She grimaced. "I didn't think about that."

"Stop looking so tragic," he said gently. "You're both free and single. Nobody's going to make snide remarks to either of you about spending an afternoon together. Is it true about the cats?" he added quickly.

"What…about the cats?"

"That they're so jealous of Kemp that visitors can't get near him," he replied.

"They weren't so bad," she confided. "Well, I did sort of get scratched by one of them. But it was just a little scratch."

"The rumor is that the more Kemp likes someone, the worse the cats are," he told her. "In which case, you'd better wear body armor if you go over there very much."

"Siamese do tend to be temperamental, I guess," she said,

wondering how many people had seen her car at Kemp's house.

"We had a dog once that hated Libby's boyfriend, when she was about fourteen," he recalled. "The dog sat and growled at him the whole time he was in the house. Then one day the boy brought him a beef bone. The next time he came over, the dog met him at the door and licked him half to death."

She pursed her lips and smiled mischievously. "I wonder if Siamese like beef bones?"

He chuckled and went on out to work.

Violet had halfway hoped that she might hear from Blake during the day. After all, they'd been lovers. But he didn't call. It was a disappointment, and her self-confidence took a nosedive. All her hopes began to drown in doubt. She went through her normal routine, answering the phone and taking messages, and typing letters for Duke Wright after he dictated them. It was a normal day. Nothing out of the ordinary. She could have cried.

Once, she almost picked up the phone and called his office. But that would never do. She couldn't look as if she were chasing him. Perhaps he just needed breathing space, in order to get used to the changed relationship between them. Surely, it was just that.

By the end of the day, she was feeling dismal. She wondered if perhaps Blake had phoned while she was briefly out of the office, because she had to run to town for Duke Wright and pick up a special delivery letter he was expecting, at the post office.

She had the opportunity to ask him as she gathered her purse and sweater to go home. He walked in with a sealed letter that needed a stamp.

"Could you drop that by the post office for me on your way home, Violet?" he asked.

"Certainly." She put on the stamp and gave him a shy glance. "Uh, there weren't any, uh, messages for me while I was gone earlier…?" she faltered.

He cocked an eyebrow and grinned. "From your ex-boss, you mean?"

She flushed. "Well…"

"There's a hard case, if ever there was one," he said. "You're taking a chance, Violet. A big one."

"Sir?"

"We all know you were out at his house," he replied easily. "News travels like wildfire around here. We've heard that those cats don't like company at all."

"They're sort of antagonistic," she confessed, without mentioning her scratches.

"Kemp took another lawyer home for supper one day and the man had to go to the emergency room. He was allergic to cat scratches."

She cleared her throat. "They are sort of possessive," she replied. "But I'm no threat. We're just friends," Violet said firmly. "He wanted to introduce me to his cats."

"That explains everything," Duke mused, grinning. "It's the cats who are interested in you, then?"

Curt Collins poked his head in the door, shamelessly eavesdropping. "And of course, Kemp loves his cats, so he brings home strangers that he thinks they'll like," he added.

"You two!" Violet exclaimed, laughing at the absurdity of it all. "I'm leaving. See you tomorrow."

They said their goodbyes and watched her go out the door.

She knew what they meant about the cats.

Mr. Kemp was a notorious loner. He never took women to his house. If he was entertaining Violet on the weekend, something was going on. She knew it was all over town if even Duke Wright knew about her visit. She wondered if the gossip had gotten back to Blake and that's why he hadn't phoned her. Of course, he could be feeling regret at his loss of control as well. She was feeling something similar. Her only excuse was that she loved him. Sadly, she knew it wasn't the same with him. Desire wasn't love.

Violet spent a sleepless night worrying about her lapse of judgment at Kemp's house, and his avoidance of her. She couldn't forget what her mother had said, about his attitude toward children. She hoped with all her heart that there wouldn't be consequences. Surely, she couldn't get pregnant from one brief interlude!

She went to work the next morning and found Duke Wright making coffee. He glanced up when she came in the door, and smiled at her.

"I've got to be out of town today. Think you can hold the office together until I get back?"

"I'll do my best, sir," she promised.

"If Kemp shows up, you can have a long lunch hour," he added with a grin. "But don't let him know I said that."

"He's not a bad man."

"You don't have my perspective on him," Duke replied quietly.

She was aware of that. Duke's divorce had been a messy one, and he blamed Kemp for his wife's unreasonable demands. She didn't say a word.

He shrugged. "Sorry. I have bad memories. I'll see you tomorrow, Violet."

"Yes, sir," she said. "Have a safe trip."

"I hope to."

She watched him walk out with a sense of foreboding. She couldn't shake the feeling that something was going on.

And it was. Kemp walked into his office and motioned Libby Collins back down the hall with him.

He told her the results of the state crime lab's autopsy on her father, which was negative.

She was relieved, and showed it.

"But the opposite was true of Violet's father," he said quietly. "Don't tell her, and don't tell Curt until I've had time to get out to Wright's ranch. I'm going to tell Violet in person and then take her home and help her break the news to her mother. It's going to be an ordeal for them. If we can catch Janet Collins, we'll charge her with first degree murder. Violet and her mother will both have to testify, and it will resurrect some terrible memories for old Mrs. Hardy. I'm not sure her heart will take it."

"What can be done?"

He shrugged. "The only thing I know is to try and reach a plea agreement, if I can talk the D.A. into it. If Janet can expect something less than life in prison, she might confess. I'll have to see. Right now, my priority is to make sure Violet doesn't hear it on the six o'clock news. There were reporters sniffing around this afternoon."

"Poor Violet," Libby said sadly. "Please, tell her if she needs me, I'll be there."

"I will. But I'm sure she knows it already. Hold down the fort for me."

"You bet."

All the way to Duke Wright's place, Kemp worried about Violet's reaction. He was still aching from their brief interlude, and he was uneasy about facing Violet again. She was a shy, introverted woman who'd had no real experience with men. He'd taken advantage of that. She might hate him for it. Just the same, he had to do what he could for her and her mother. It wasn't going to be easy for either of them to face the fact that Mr. Hardy had been murdered.

* * *

Violet was just finishing the last of the new cattle herd files when she heard footsteps coming into her office.

She looked up, and her heart jumped wildly as she saw Blake Kemp for the first time since their passionate afternoon. She colored furiously as he came into the room and paused just in front of her desk. He looked very elegant in a pale gray vested suit, not a hair out of place. His blue eyes were quiet and sympathetic as they met hers.

"Is something wrong?" she asked at once, uneasy because of the way he looked.

"Yes, Violet," he replied. "We have to speak to your mother. Will Wright let you leave early?"

"He's not here today," she faltered. She stood up. "What's happened?"

"We just got the results back on your father's autopsy. He was poisoned, Violet. It wasn't a natural death. It was murder."

Murder. *Murder.* She felt the blood draining out of her face. Janet Collins had killed her father.

"That woman," she bit off. "That damned, greedy woman killed my father!"

He moved around the desk quickly and pulled her into his arms, wrapping her up tight. "It's all right," he murmured softly at her ear, contracting his arms when she began to shiver. "We'll make her pay for it. I swear we will."

She'd felt shock and then anger. Now she felt grief well up in her like water behind a dam. She'd loved her father, despite his faults. How in the world was her mother going to react to the news?

"It will kill Mama," she choked, sliding her arms around Blake's waist.

"No, it won't," he assured her. "She's stronger than she

looks. But I think you and I should both break the news to her."

"Yes. Thank you," she added belatedly.

He drew in a long breath. Odd, how right she felt in his arms. He'd ached for her for the past few days. This was like coming home.

She loved the comfort of his embrace. Except for her mother, she'd had little real affection in her life. It was wonderful to melt into his muscular body and let him absorb all her worries, all her fears. He made her feel secure, protected.

His hand smoothed over her hair, enjoying its softness.

Footsteps interrupted them. Curt came into the room, stopped dead, and started to go back out again, faintly embarrassed.

Blake saw him and released Violet. "She's had some bad news," he told the other man. "It will be all over town soon enough, so you might as well know now. Her father was poisoned."

"By my stepmother?" Curt asked miserably.

Blake nodded. "Very probably."

Curt grimaced. "Violet, I'm so sorry."

She wiped her eyes with the back of her hand. They felt swollen and hot. "It's not your fault, Curt," she said sadly. "You and Libby have suffered because of her, too. We're all victims."

"And we can't find her," Curt muttered angrily.

"We will," Blake said firmly. "I swear we will."

"Is there anything I can do?" Curt asked.

Violet shook her head. "But thanks anyway. We're going to tell Mama. I hope it isn't going to be too much for her."

Blake smiled faintly as Violet went to gather up her things. "I think you'll find that your mother is going to want vengeance more than sympathy when she knows the truth."

Violet smiled. "I hope so," she replied. "I really hope that's how she's going to feel."

Blake turned to Curt. "I'm going to follow Violet home. If Wright calls, can you tell him what's going on?"

"He left his foreman in charge," Curt replied. "I'll make sure he knows. There's nothing that can't wait until tomorrow. Violet, if you need anything, all you have to do is tell us. I know Libby would tell you the same thing."

"Thanks, Curt," she replied, managing a smile as she joined Blake. "I'm ready when you are," she told him.

"Let's go." Blake stood aside to let her go out the door first.

Mrs. Hardy looked up expectantly, and with faint surprise, when she saw Blake come in the door with her daughter. Both of them wore somber expressions.

She was propped up on the sofa with pillows. She gave them a wise look. "You have the results of the autopsy," she guessed. "That floozie poisoned my husband, didn't she?" she added, eyes flashing. "I want her drawn and quartered!"

Blake smiled at Violet. "Didn't I tell you?" he mused.

Violet nodded. "Yes, you did." She put down her things and went to sit beside her mother on the sofa and pull her close. "We're going to find her and send her away for years and years," she promised her mother. "It's just a matter of time and evidence."

"Evidence being the key word," Blake agreed. "Fortunately, the criminalists who processed the scene did a thorough job. They couldn't rule out homicide, so they did a good job of collecting trace evidence. There's more than enough for a DNA profile. If Janet was in that room, we'll be able to prove it. There's also an eyewitness who saw her come out of the room shortly before your husband was discovered," he added.

"Yes, but we don't know where she is," Violet murmured.

"Oh, that's just a minor detail," Blake said carelessly. "I

have a private detective tracking her. It's just a matter of time."

"You didn't say anything about that," Violet remarked.

"Finding Janet is essential to Libby and Curt. They're fighting to keep their ranch, and it's not going well," he said grimly. "Janet has done everything in her power to take it away from them. She's absconded with all the money and tied up their finances so that they can hardly pay bills. They need her found, and quickly. So do both of you," he added. "The longer this drags on, the worse it's going to get."

"How can a human being be so cold?" Mrs. Hardy wondered out loud, her delicate features drawn as she spoke. "Money isn't that important."

"To some people it is," Blake replied. "I've seen men go to prison for life because they stole less than twenty dollars. A thief doesn't know how much money his victim is carrying, as a rule. Sometimes the victim resists, and dies, and the thief ends up with pocket change and a life sentence. Greed is its own punishment."

"I hope Janet Collins gets hers," Violet said quietly, hugging her mother. She glanced at Blake. "I suppose it will be in all the papers?"

"Undoubtedly," he agreed. He moved into the living room and dropped down into a comfortable armchair. "Personal tragedies have become popular entertainment. We've reached an all-time low in journalistic ethics."

"Where do you think Janet Collins went?" Mrs. Hardy asked abruptly.

Blake crossed his long legs and leaned back in the chair. "At a guess, somewhere close by. She won't want to let go of the ranch. Libby and Curt have had some threats already, probably at her instigation."

"I'm sorry they're having such trouble," Violet said. "Libby's the best friend I have."

"I won't give up until Janet is found," Blake assured her. "I've got one of the best private investigators in Texas on the job."

Mrs. Hardy was dabbing at her eyes. Anger had given way to grief. "I wondered about the coroner's report, saying that he had a heart attack," she murmured aloud. "He'd had all sorts of tests, and there was no trace of heart trouble."

"From what the medical examiner told me, the poison paralyzes the heart. Essentially, it stops it dead. Since no one suspected foul play, they didn't bother with an autopsy. But I credit those investigators in San Antonio with doing a great job of evidence gathering. When we finally catch Janet, we'll have enough to hang her."

Violet hugged her mother. "It will be all right," she said, although she didn't really feel it.

"The newspapers will have a field day, won't they?" Mrs. Hardy asked suddenly, her face contorted.

"We'll get through it," Violet assured her. "We're tough, aren't we?"

Mrs. Hardy hesitated, then she smiled. "Yes, dear. We're tough."

"We'll find a way around the publicity," Blake told them. "First things first. We have to find Janet."

"Thank you for coming with Violet to give me the news, Blake," Mrs. Hardy told him gently. "It made it easier."

"I thought it might," he said gently. "I'm sorry it turned out this way," he added.

"So are we," Violet replied. "But we don't get to choose our obstacles, do we?"

"How true," Mrs. Hardy murmured. She looked toward Blake. "Would you like to come to dinner?"

Violet flushed. She knew her mother was trying to play matchmaker, but she wished she hadn't. She was uneasy around Blake. She didn't know what he expected of her. She didn't know how she should behave.

Blake saw her indecision and averted his gaze to Mrs. Hardy. "Thanks," he said, "but I've got a lot of work to get through tonight for a client." The client was Libby Collins, but he wasn't going to discuss that with the women.

"Another time," Mrs. Hardy suggested.

"Another time," he agreed pleasantly. "I'd better get on the road. If you need me, call," he told Violet firmly.

"Of course, we will," she said without looking directly at him, and with a forced smile.

"My interim secretary is getting married," he remarked. "You might consider coming back to work. Libby and Mabel miss you."

Violet was surprised, because he hadn't been in touch with her since their dinner. She didn't even know that he'd hired an interim secretary. He sounded as if he wanted Violet to come back. But he didn't look desperate.

On the other hand, she missed seeing him every day. It was a wrench to work for Duke Wright. It guaranteed that she wouldn't see Blake on a regular basis at all. Today had been a rare event.

"Think about it, at least," Blake added quietly.

"Yes," she replied. "I certainly will."

He studied her for a few seconds too long, his eyes narrow and intent. She might mistake his invitation for something romantic, but that wasn't the case at all. He felt guilty for what he'd let happen at his house. Violet could be pregnant. He didn't dare keep his distance until he knew for sure. The woman hadn't a clue about relationships, and she'd be in a hell of a fix if she really had become pregnant.

He had to keep her close so that he'd know, whatever her condition turned out to be. If there was going to be a child...

He stopped the thought dead. He wouldn't think about that

consequence. He had to look on the bright side. He wasn't ready for marriage and a family. He might never be. Certainly, Violet was hardly the sort of woman he envisioned marrying. She was sweet and kind, but she wasn't assertive. There were divisions between them that she didn't understand. He couldn't hurt her by pointing them out.

He had to bide his time until he knew for sure if there was going to be a child. That wasn't her fault, either. He'd seduced her, out of loneliness and aching hunger. He still felt the need for her. It was why he'd avoided her for the past couple of days. He'd hoped to get it under control.

But it wasn't. He looked at her and he wanted her. His body was already as taut as drawn rope, just from looking at her. He knew instinctively that if he touched her, he wasn't going to be able to pull away. The pleasure she'd given him was exquisite. He wanted it again. And he didn't dare have it.

"Violet, why don't you walk Blake out?" Mrs. Hardy suggested when there was a brief silence.

"I can find my way out," Blake said without making a big thing of Violet's hesitation. He even smiled. "Think about the job," he suggested. "We make a good team…you and me and Libby and Mabel," he added just when she thought he was talking about the two of them.

She nodded. "I will think about it," she promised.

"I'll be in touch," he replied. He didn't say goodbye. He simply left.

"See, dear, he misses you!" Mrs. Hardy exclaimed when they heard his car start up outside. "He wants you back! You'll do it, won't you?"

"I have to change clothes and get supper started," she interrupted to halt her mother's speculation. "What would you like? How about pancakes?"

"Pancakes? For supper?" the older woman exclaimed.

"Why not? We love pancakes!"

Mrs. Hardy smiled. "Then pancakes it is. And coffee."

Coffee reminded Violet of Blake and made her sad. She'd lost her job over coffee. But she didn't let it show. "Decaf for you," she teased, and went to change her clothes.

Seven

Blake spent the weekend working, trying to keep his mind off Violet. Monday morning, his private investigator called with some good news for Libby and Curt Collins. Their father's priceless coin collection had been located at a dealer's shop in San Antonio. There were bankbooks. There was also a copy of a new will, about which Blake had some suspicions. Blake phoned the dealer and arranged to drive up the following morning early and collect the coins and the documents. He told the dealer that he'd have Libby phone him as soon as she came to work—she could vouch for the fact that Blake was her attorney and authorized to handle her inheritance.

He didn't know if Janet Collins was aware of the coin collection's whereabouts and he considered that he might need backup.

He phoned the chief of police's office and talked to Cash Grier, who agreed to drive up with him. Grier would intimidate most people with evil intentions, Blake thought humorously, even without a firearm.

He told Libby about the trip and also asked her to go by Violet's house that afternoon with a pizza and cheer the women up. He also suggested that it wouldn't hurt for Libby to mention how badly they missed her in the office, and how short-handed they were since the interim secretary, Jessie, had given notice and quit. Libby laughingly agreed.

Libby was surprised at Violet's new look and her nervousness when she stopped by Violet's house after work. She'd known Violet for a long time. She'd never known her to be anything except calm and collected.

"Mr. Kemp asked me to tell you how much we're missing you," Libby said, tongue-in-cheek.

Violet laughed softly. "Are you really, or are you just short-handed because Jessie quit without finishing out her notice?"

Libby's eyes widened. "How in the world did you know that?"

Violet chuckled. "Mrs. Landers who works at the newspaper office," she replied. "She's the best gossip we have, and she thought I'd like to know that poor Mr. Blake was short a secretary. She saw the baby shower announcement that Jessie brought in and Jessie mentioned that she was leaving the job early because Mr. Kemp was hopeful that his old secretary might come back if she knew how hard-pressed he was for help."

"Well!" Libby exclaimed on a laugh, showing her the box of hot pizza. "It's all true, of course. I brought you and Mrs. Hardy a pizza."

"You can have some, too, Libby, since you were nice enough to bring it," Violet said, hugging the other woman. "It was sweet of you. Mama and I have had a bad day."

"Mr. Kemp told me about it," Libby replied. "I'm so sorry."

Violet shrugged. "We all have hard times. We'll get through ours. It's just that it's brought back so many terrible memories."

"All my stepmother's fault," Libby said coldly. "Curt and I would love to get our hands on her!"

"Take a number and get in line," Violet mused with morbid humor.

"I see your point."

"Come on into the kitchen, and I'll find some plates. Mama, Libby's here, and she brought a pizza," she called to her mother in the living room.

"Hello, Libby," Mrs. Hardy called back. "That was sweet of you!"

"That's just what I said, Mama," Violet teased.

She led Libby into the kitchen.

"One way or another, my stepmother has made some terrible problems for all of us," Libby said somberly. "But she messed up."

"How?"

"My dad must have suspected something, because he made a new will and left it with a rare coin dealer in San Antonio," Libby replied. "The coin collection he had is there, too. Mr. Kemp says Curt and I will be able to pay off our mortgage and get our livestock back."

"Libby, that's wonderful!" Violet exclaimed.

"Yes. Wonderful. But Julie Merrill has been making my life hell lately. She's got her claws into Jordan and she won't let go. He thinks I'm just jealous and trying to break them up. But it's more than that," she said grimly. "She's dangerous. She's been spreading all sorts of rumors about Calhoun Ballenger. He got Mr. Kemp to file suit against her for slander."

"Good for Calhoun!"

Libby helped put pizza on plates. "I thought Jordan cared about me," she said miserably. "But the minute Julie turned on the charm, he dropped me flat. He even let her insult me without saying a single word in my defense."

"I'm really sorry," Violet told her. "I thought Jordan was smart enough to see through her."

"She's pretty and smart and rich," Libby murmured.

"And what are you, hideous?" Violet chided. "Your people were founding families of Jacobsville, and you're a paralegal. You're pretty, too. You're worth two of Julie Merrill."

Libby looked less stressed. She smiled. "Thanks, Violet. I really have missed you," she added. "I don't have anybody else that I can talk to, except my brother, and I couldn't tell him how I really feel about Jordan."

"Julie will fall into that deep hole she's digging one day," Violet told the other woman. "With any luck, Janet will fall into one just as deep!" She hesitated, remembering what Libby had said. "Mr. Kemp isn't going to go up there alone to get those things, is he? I mean, Janet might have an accomplice…"

"Cash Grier is going with him," Libby interrupted.

Violet laughed. "I'll stop worrying right now. Nobody is going to mess with our chief of police."

"That's gospel," Libby agreed. "Although you might remember that Mr. Kemp was an officer in the reserves until just recently. He's no shrinking daisy."

"I know," Violet replied, smiling. "Remember those two men he threw out of our office?"

"I'm trying to forget!"

They both laughed.

The pizza was delicious. Violet walked out with Libby when she was ready to leave.

"Are you going to come back?" Libby asked the other woman seriously.

"Yes," Violet said. "I dread having to tell Mr. Wright, though," she added. "He was kind to me."

"Duke's nice. He won't mind. He may not like Mr. Kemp, but he likes you," she added with a smile. "I'll bet he won't even ask you to work a two week notice."

"That would be nice." She wrapped her arms around herself. The night was cool. "Has Mr. Kemp really missed me?"

Libby smiled. "He really has. He's set new records for hostility and impatience. I think Jessie quit because she reached the end of her rope. She couldn't please the boss no matter what she did. It seemed to Mabel and me that Mr. Kemp was trying to make her leave."

Violet smiled delightedly. "I've missed him, too," she confessed.

Libby hugged her. "We all know how you feel about him. I think you've got a good chance with him, Violet," she said gently. "I wouldn't encourage you to come back if I didn't. I know too much about unrequited love."

"You and Jordan are going to work out one day, too," Violet assured her friend. "I'm sure of it."

"Chance would be a fine thing," Libby sighed. "Well, I'd better get home. Curt's having a night out with the boys so I don't have to worry about his supper, thank goodness."

"Your brother's a nice man."

"He is, isn't he?" Libby grinned. "I wouldn't have minded you for a sister-in-law, you know. But you can't get past love. I know. I've tried."

"It will work out, Libby," Violet told her.

"Somehow," Libby agreed.

"Thanks for the pizza and the company."

"You're very welcome."

"I'll call Mr. Wright tonight," Violet added, full of excitement.

"We'll look forward to having you back whenever you can come," Libby called on her way to the car.

* * *

Violet did phone Duke Wright, and he did waive her two weeks' notice. He was sorry to lose her, he added, but a blind man could see how she felt about Kemp. Not that Kemp deserved her, he added wryly. Violet thanked him and hung up. She was going to be sitting at her desk when Mr. Kemp came in the next morning. She could hardly wait to see the look on his face!

Kemp and Cash Grier were on their way back from San Antonio after a stop at the coin dealer's shop, a local attorney's office, and a quick lunch. Kemp had salvaged more than enough of the late Riddle Collins's assets to save Libby and Curt Collins from bankruptcy. They'd be able to pay off their outstanding loan and have plenty left over to put in the bank. The coin collection their father had left them was worth a fortune by itself. But in addition to it, Kemp had found two savings accounts and a new will that their late father had placed with the coin dealer in San Antonio. Apparently, he hadn't trusted his wife, Janet, one bit, and had planned for her legal shenanigans after his death. He'd assured that his children wouldn't be left penniless.

"Isn't greed amazing?" Kemp murmured aloud, having told Grier the bare bones of the shameful way Janet had treated her stepchildren.

"It is," Grier said. "I've never understood it. I like having enough to provide a roof over my head and the occasional night at the theater, but there are plenty of things I wouldn't consider doing even to make myself rich."

"Same here." Kemp glanced at the older man curiously.

"Something bothering you?" Grier asked.

"I'm surprised at the way you've fit in here," he replied with a faint smile. "You do know the whole town's talking about your defense of your two patrol officers—the ones the mayor is trying to fire."

"I like controversy if it's in a good cause," Grier said. He grinned. "I'm not letting them fire good officers for doing their jobs."

"You've got some drug traffickers on the run as well," Kemp mused. "You're shaking up our little community. I like the changes. So do a lot of other people."

"I'm glad, but I didn't take the job to win a popularity contest."

"Why did you?" Kemp asked evenly.

Grier sighed. "I'm tired of living on the run," he confessed, gazing out the window while Kemp drove. "I'm feeling my age. I think I might put down roots here."

"With Tippy?" Kemp fished.

Grier didn't fly at him, as he'd expected. The older man frowned slightly. "She's not what she seems," he replied quietly. "I've misjudged her badly. I don't know that she'd be willing to take me on, once she's back on her feet and able to work again. In any case, I can't let her far out of my sight right now. Not until that third kidnapper is in custody," he added coldly. "If he turns up in Jacobsville and makes a try for her, he'd better carry life insurance."

"It would take a stupid criminal to do that."

"I've locked up a lot of guys who aren't rocket scientists," Grier said drolly, with a speaking glance at Kemp.

Kemp chuckled. "I've defended a fair number who weren't, too," he had to agree. "Which reminds me, if you want me to defend your patrol officers at the hearing, I'll do it pro bono."

"Thanks," Grier told him. "But I've got a big surprise for the city council when they meet for that hearing."

"I forgot. You're related to the Hart boys, aren't you?"

Grier grinned. "They're my cousins."

"And Simon Hart is our state attorney general," he added,

laughing. "Then I don't need to offer my services. I won't try to guess who you're bringing with you."

"You won't need to guess," Grier said. He stretched lazily. "I need a few days off. Once the election is over and the disciplinary hearing is decided, I'm going to take some time off. Tippy's little brother is coming down here soon. He likes to fish. Maybe he and I can stake out a riverbank for a few hours and take some fresh fish home to Tippy for dinner."

"Can she cook?" Kemp asked, surprised.

"Indeed she can," he replied. "You'd be amazed at how domestic she is." His eyes were soft. "She looks right at home in a kitchen. I could get used to seeing her across a table for the rest of my life."

Kemp felt uneasy. Grier, an older and lonelier man than himself, was apparently thinking solemnly about a stable and shared future with a woman. Kemp thought of marriage and it made him uncomfortable.

"I'm not in the market for a wife," Kemp said aloud. "I like my own space, my own company."

Grier gave him a grin. "I used to be that way, too. There's always the one woman who can change your mind."

Kemp shrugged. "Not for me. I've been that route once. I never want to go over the same ground again."

"Nothing wrong with being a loner," Grier said. "Until recent days, I felt that way, too."

"Tippy's a beauty."

"She's got a good brain, and she's a quick hand in an emergency," Grier told him. "It's not about looks."

"Sorry," Kemp said belatedly. "I was thinking out loud."

"I hear your new secretary quit," Grier mused.

"She couldn't spell," Kemp muttered. "It's no loss."

"What are you going to do, have Libby and Mabel double up on work again?"

"Violet might come back."

Grier pursed his lips. "I thought she was keen on having you for a barbecue as the entrée."

Kemp shrugged. "We're speaking again." He tried not to let it show that they were doing a lot more than that.

"If you say so."

"I can get another secretary whenever I need one," Kemp added doggedly.

"Does the employment agency know this?"

Kemp gave him a glare. "Just because they hung up on me doesn't mean they don't want my business."

"I'm sure."

"Anyway, if Violet comes back, all my problems will be solved," he said. "And now that I've got Riddle Collins's secret stash in that suitcase, Libby and Curt Collins will be out of debt and back in their own home again."

"That won't suit Julie Merrill," Grier murmured coolly. "She's hot after Jordan Powell's money. Poor Libby."

"Poor Julie, if you can get her where we all want her," Kemp said.

"I'm working on that," Grier assured him. "One way or another, I'm going to put the last of the drug cartel out of business in Jacobsville."

"With my blessing," Kemp replied, smiling.

Kemp came into his office early the next morning with Riddle's stash and showed it to Libby, who'd come in early for the occasion. She was ecstatic as they went over the proof of her father's love for her and Curt.

A few minutes later, Kemp started out for the courthouse to file the revised will Riddle had left. When he walked into the outer office, the first thing he saw was Violet, sitting at her desk.

His expression was enough to feed Violet's hungry heart. She smiled, flushed and beamed up at him.

"You said I could come back," she reminded him brightly.

"Yes, I did," he replied, smiling. "Are you staying?"

She nodded.

"How about making a fresh pot of coffee?" he asked.

"Regular?"

"Half and half," he replied, averting his eyes. "Too much caffeine isn't good for me."

He went out the door, leaving Violet with her jaw dropping.

"I told you he missed you!" Libby whispered mischievously as she followed the boss onto the sidewalk.

As the day went on, Kemp found himself looking for excuses to go to the front of his office. He went through two pots of coffee, because that was the best excuse he had. Violet was wearing a sassy blue dress that emphasized her nice, rounded figure. It was fairly low cut in front, and with her frosted dark hair and her improved use of makeup, she was enough to turn any man's head.

Libby and Mabel noticed his sudden interest in the coffeepot with subdued humor. They didn't want to embarrass Violet, who flushed every time the boss came close.

It was almost inevitable that Violet stayed just a few minutes longer than Mabel and Libby at the end of the day.

She tidied up her desk and slowly gathered her purse and sweater. Blake came out to the front office and stood, openly staring at her, with his hands in his pockets and an odd, intent look in the blue eyes behind his trendy spectacles.

"Are you in a rush to get home? Can you phone your mother and tell her you'll be a few minutes late?" he added.

"Of…of course," she stammered. The way he was looking at her made her tingle from head to toe. She fumbled the phone to her ear and dialed, her eyes eating her handsome boss all the while.

She told her mother she'd be a few minutes late, trying not to react obviously to her parent's amusement.

Blake held out his hand. Violet dropped her purse and sweater on her chair and went to him, letting him lead her back to his office.

He closed the door and pulled her hungrily into his arms. She sighed with pure delight as his hard mouth found her lips and he lifted her into an even more intimate embrace.

"I've missed you," he ground out against her responsive lips.

"I've missed you...too," she whispered back.

"Come home with me," he suggested huskily.

She knew what he was really suggesting, and it wasn't supper. She wanted to go with him. She wanted to be with him. But she was hesitant.

He felt her hesitation. He let her slide down his hard body and he stared into her eyes hungrily. "Well?"

She swallowed. Her gaze was on his broad chest, because she couldn't look him in the eye and refuse him.

"What are you offering me, Blake?" she asked quietly.

He scowled. "Are we bargaining for sex?"

She stared up at him, dumbfounded. "Is that all you want from me?"

He was confused. Usually logical and cool in his thinking, now he was like a young man on the brink of his first affair.

"I don't want to get married, Violet," he said gently. "You know that."

She swallowed hard. "Yes. You've already said that. But I don't want to be your mistress."

His jaw tensed. "I don't recall asking you to be."

"What would you call it, then?" Violet asked sadly. "You want to sleep with me, with no ties, isn't that the truth?"

He stuck his hands in his slacks pockets and let out a long sigh.

"My mother is old-fashioned," she continued. "She raised me to think of sex as something that goes hand in hand with love and marriage. It would break her heart to have me settle for a purely physical liaison with any man, especially you." She looked up at him miserably. "Jacobsville is a small town, Blake. Everybody would know."

"I'm not a slave to public opinion," he said harshly, feeling himself lose ground.

"Yes, but I am," she replied. She stepped back, feeling a sudden coldness in his manner. It wasn't what she'd expected when she came in here with him. She'd hoped that he might come to love her. They'd been so close at his house. Now they were like strangers.

He was furious. He was confused. This woman had caused him more inner turmoil than he'd known since the death of his fiancée, years before. He loved his freedom. But he hated the thought of losing Violet.

"Violet," he began slowly, "I was engaged once. I loved her more than life. After I lost her, I didn't want to go on living." He frowned. "I…can't go through that again."

She looked up into his turbulent eyes. "Why would you have to? You don't love me," she said miserably. "You only want me."

She turned and went to the door.

Before she could open it, his hand covered hers on the doorknob. "Wait."

"I should never have returned here to work," she said. "I'll go back to Mr. Wright. You can get another temporary secretary to fill in until you replace me."

"No!"

Tears blurred her blue eyes. She'd never been so miserable in her life. "Just let me go, please!"

He moved his hand. Seconds later, she was out the front door and gone. He stood alone in his office, feeling empty and cold. She wanted something he couldn't give her. Why couldn't women be like men, he wondered angrily, and just enjoy the present without asking for solemn vows of forever?

He went home in a snit and made supper for himself and the cats. They gave him odd looks, as if they sensed his inner turmoil.

He glared at them. "Don't you start," he muttered. Mee rubbed against his legs. Yow sat watching him with blue accusing eyes. "Great," he muttered. "Now I'm talking to cats!"

He finished his meager supper and tried to get interested in a television program, but his body ached with thoughts of Violet in his arms. He wasn't giving in, though. If she thought she'd get him in front of a minister by holding out physically, she was dead wrong.

He couldn't forget their one time of intimacy, the beauty and joy of possessing her. It had been a perfect physical interlude.

Then he remembered something else he'd tried to forget. They'd had unprotected sex. What if Violet got pregnant?

He sat up straight, his eyes wide and stunned at just the thought. What would they do? He knew for a fact that Violet would never be able to go to a clinic. She'd insist on having the child. He had a horror of children. He'd never gotten over the fact that Shannon had been carrying his child when she died. It had warped his attitude toward pregnancy. He thought of children and he remembered how he felt when he knew his child had died with the woman he loved. It brought back nightmares of pain. Violet wouldn't understand that. She wanted happily ever after. All he wanted was relief from the nagging physical hunger that was taking him over.

But if she was pregnant, he couldn't desert her. Not only would it be unworthy of him as a man, it would reflect badly on his character in a town the size of Jacobsville. The gossip would ruin Violet's reputation and the shame might well kill her mother, considering Mrs. Hardy's fragile health.

He cursed under his breath. If he'd never invited Violet home with him, none of this would ever have happened. Why couldn't he have just let her go and left it at that? He'd landed them in hell with his uncontrollable passion. He couldn't blame that on Violet. All the same, he didn't know what he was going to do.

But he couldn't let her quit. Not until he knew about her condition. He picked up the phone and punched in her number.

Violet had managed to hide her misery from her mother. She knew that Blake wouldn't mind if she quit again. It would probably be a relief to him. He wanted her and he couldn't have her on his terms. Perhaps it would make things easier if she went back to work for Duke. She should pick up the phone and call him, right now...

The phone rang, making her jump. She picked it up without thinking.

"Hello?" she said.

"Don't quit," Blake said quietly.

Her heart jumped up into her throat. "Excuse me?" she stammered.

"Let's take it one day at a time, Violet. All right?" he asked, and he actually sounded as if he was rethinking the future.

She felt reborn. Her spirit soared. She could hardly contain the happiness she felt. "All right," she said on a soft laugh. "One day at a time!"

Eight

For days, Violet and Blake were hesitant around each other. He was the soul of courtesy. He didn't curse or yell. He didn't throw anyone out of the office. He seemed to be a changed man.

Violet loved the tenderness he showed her. He never raised his voice or made sarcastic comments about her work. But he wasn't forward in any way, either, and he didn't touch her. He seemed to be waiting for something, watching. Violet wondered why.

Julie Merrill was arrested for the attempted arson of Libby and Curt Collins's house the following Saturday, and Cash Grier had a big surprise for the city council at the Monday disciplinary hearing. The patrol officers were exonerated and the mayor was embarrassed for trying to force them to retract drunk driving charges against his uncle, State Senator Merrill.

The next day was the primary elections. Calhoun Ballenger won the Democratic nomination away from Senator Merrill in a huge upset, and the mayor lost his job in a special election won by former mayor Eddie Cane. It was a great day for Jacobsville.

But on Wednesday morning, Violet lost her breakfast at the office. Blake, walking past the bathroom, heard her retching. He felt sick himself. Violet was healthy as a horse. If she was throwing up, there could only be one explanation. She had to be pregnant.

It was the end of the world. Blake went around for the rest of the day in a daze. So did Violet. He overheard Mabel and Libby murmuring about Violet's bout of sickness and her upcoming doctor's appointment. They clammed up immediately when Blake walked into the room. It didn't take much to figure out that if Violet was pregnant, her boss was responsible. After all, who else had Violet been crazy about for a year? More importantly, who had she been alone with lately? It didn't take a lot of guesswork.

Violet was panic-stricken after she lost her breakfast. She phoned Dr. Lou Coltrain's office and made an appointment, all too aware that Mabel and Libby could hear her doing it. She told them she thought she had a virus and she was afraid of giving it to her mother. But they were suspicious and it showed.

She drove to Lou's office after work, leaving Libby and Mabel to close up. She swore Dr. Coltrain to secrecy before she even mentioned her symptoms. Lou gave her a worried look as she had her nurse draw blood for a simple pregnancy test.

"One time," Violet choked when Lou gave her the results of the test a few minutes later.

"One time is all it takes," Lou said ruefully. "Oh, Violet."

"What am I going to do?" the younger woman groaned, with her face in her hands. "I can't even step on ants, Lou!"

The other woman patted her shoulder sympathetically. "I'm sure once Blake knows…"

Violet gave her a horrified look.

"Who else could it be?" Lou asked reasonably. "He's the only man you care about, and you spent half a day at his house," she added, smiling ruefully when Violet flushed. "Well, on the positive side, it won't be difficult to find your due date."

"He doesn't want children," Violet said. "He doesn't even want anything permanent. He said so…!"

Lou eased her back down into the chair she'd bolted from. "Don't panic."

"My mother has already had a stroke! She raised me to be good…!"

"People are human," Lou interrupted. "Your mother isn't going to disown you or throw you out into the street."

"Everyone will know," Violet groaned. She drew in a shaky breath. "I could move up to San Antonio," she began.

"That would make it even worse," Lou assured her. "And leave Blake to face the music all alone." She pursed her lips and her dark eyes flashed. "Maybe that's not such a bad thing. I thought better of him. He's intelligent enough to know about using protection. He couldn't have thought you were experienced!"

The flush got worse. "Am I wearing a sign?"

"It's a small town," Lou pointed out. "You aren't promiscuous."

Violet drew in another breath. "I don't know what to do."

"Go home and eat healthy. I'll prescribe vitamins. You need to be in the care of a good OB/GYN specialist as well. I know one in Victoria I can send you to," she added when Violet looked even more terrified. "She's discreet."

Violet ground her teeth together. "This isn't how I planned my life."

"Life is what happens when you make other plans," Lou quoted. She frowned. "I don't remember who said that, but it's absolutely true." She gave Violet a long, smiling look. "You'll make a wonderful mother."

A mother! In the terror of the moment, Violet had lost track of things. But now she realized that there would be a miniature version of herself or Blake. She felt…odd. Her hands went to her flat stomach in wonder. There was a baby inside her!

"Now you're getting the picture." Lou laughed. "There's nothing quite like the feeling a woman gets when she realizes there's a tiny life inside her body. When I knew I was pregnant, I could hardly believe it," she added. "I was excited, and then afraid, and then I walked around in a daze of daydreams." Her eyes misted. "It was the happiest nine months of my life. I can hardly wait to do it all over again, but we wanted to wait until our little boy was older. It's hard to handle a baby and a toddler and a profession, all at the same time."

Violet smiled, feeling torn by emotions. "I've always wanted children. I just hoped…well, I'd have liked being married."

"Tell Blake and you will be," Lou suggested.

Violet shook her head. "I can't tell him. Not now. Maybe not ever."

"He has an obligation to help support his child, Violet," Lou said firmly. "You didn't get pregnant all by yourself. As for keeping it from him, that isn't going to be possible. Not in a town this small. For one thing," she said, "when you get this prescription filled, everybody in the pharmacy is going to know what's going on," she added, writing it out. "It's for prenatal vitamins."

Violet had that base covered, at least. "I'll drive up to Victoria and get it filled," she said doggedly.

"All right, ostrich, hide your head in the sand while you can," Lou said amusedly.

"I can do this," she said firmly.

"Sure you can," Lou humored her. She handed Violet the prescription. "No heavy lifting for the first trimester. And get plenty of sleep."

"Plenty of sleep. Right," Violet muttered, foreseeing sleeplessness that might never end, from worrying about her condition and her mother's health.

Lou patted her shoulder. "You won't believe me, but in five or six months, you're going to look back on this day and smile."

"If I were a gambler, I'd take you up on that," Violet said heavily. "But thanks, Dr. Lou."

Lou watched her go with worried eyes that Violet didn't see. She wondered how in the world Violet was going to manage.

Blake knew that Violet had been to see Lou Coltrain because he'd seen her coming out of Lou's office on his way home from work. The visit, combined with the hunted look on Violet's face when she came in to work the next day, told the whole story. He cursed himself for what he'd done to them both. If he'd kept his head, if he'd used protection, if, if, if…! Now he was going to be a father and he had to marry the mother of his child or disgrace himself and Mrs. Hardy as well as Violet. He hated the whole idea of giving up his freedom. He hated the idea of a child in his life. He wasn't family man material.

But he was a responsible man and he had a conscience. He was going to have to act. He didn't want Violet doing something desperate.

If he told her that he knew about her condition, she'd know that he was asking her to marry him out of duty and she'd refuse. So he had to hide his real feelings and pretend to have a change of heart while there was still time. He had a poker face. He could pull it off. After all, what choice did he have?

When it was quitting time, he went out to the main office. "Violet, how about a cup of coffee and a steak and salad at Barbara's Café?" he asked carelessly. "You can take a salad home to your mother."

Libby and Mabel hid delighted smiles, said their good-nights, and left at once to give the couple some privacy.

Violet stared at her boss curiously. "Supper? With you?" she stammered.

He forced a smile. "Supper with me. Are you game?"

"People will talk."

He shrugged. "So?"

She felt a little better. At least he liked her enough that he wasn't backing away from gossip. Maybe there was a little hope for the future after all. She smiled. "I'd love to!"

"Good. Call your mother and we'll walk over to Barbara's after we lock up."

"I'll do it right now!"

Barbara served three meals a day, and her café was always crowded after quitting time. Today was no exception. When Violet walked in with Blake Kemp, conversation muted at once and all eyes turned toward the couple in the buffet line.

They chose steaks and salads, and Violet placed an order to go for her mother. But she insisted on paying for her own order, to Blake's dismay.

"Talk about independent women," Blake murmured dryly as they sat down to eat.

"Mama raised me that way," Violet said simply, smiling. "She said we need to depend on ourselves and not impose on other people."

"I never thought of steak as an imposition," he mused.

She laughed. "Thanks for the offer, anyway," she replied.

He finished his salad in short order and started on his steak. He didn't use condiments. He noticed that Violet didn't, either.

"What sort of music do you like?" he asked abruptly.

She hesitated with a piece of steak halfway to her mouth. "I like country-western and classical. And some hard rock," she added impishly.

He laughed. "Actually, so do I."

"Do you like to read?"

He nodded. "I like ancient history and biographies."

She smiled sheepishly. "I like women's fiction and books about gardening and gourmet cooking."

He searched her eyes. "Your mother said you like astronomy."

"I do," she agreed. "But I can't afford a telescope."

He leaned forward. "I have a twelve-inch Schmidt-Cassegrain."

That was an expensive composite telescope, part refractor and part reflector. She'd dreamed of owning something so large and efficient. She gasped. "You do?"

He laughed. "I spend a lot of time outside at night. Since I live so far out of town, I don't have problems with light pollution."

"I'll bet you can see the craters on the moon," she sighed.

"I can see inside them," he corrected.

She whistled softly. "I'd love to look through it."

"We can arrange that. Think you could get used to two warlike Siamese cats?"

"I like Mee and Yow," she replied, curious.

He stared down at his plate. "I've been giving a lot of thought to our situation," he said finally. "Since you left and went to work for Wright, my priorities have changed. I'm not as happy being alone as I used to be."

She put down her fork and sat just staring at him. Her heart was beating her to death. Could he mean...?

He lifted his eyes to hers. "I said that I wasn't a marrying man. And at the time, I believed it. But I like having you around." His gaze fell to her mouth and his eyes darkened. "In fact, I'd like having you around more than just at work."

"I don't understand," she faltered.

He reached for her hand and curled her fingers into his. He looked into her blue eyes and felt as if he were drowning. "I think we might get engaged," he said, trying to find the right words and failing miserably.

"You and me?" she exclaimed.

"You and me," he agreed. He slid his fingers over hers. "Violet, we have a lot in common. I think we'll find a lot more as we go along." His voice lowered. "And physically, there's no question of compatibility."

She flushed softly. "But, you said you didn't ever want to get married, and that you'd never want children..."

"A man says a lot of stupid things when he's trying to hold on to a comfortable routine, Violet," he replied. "I'm a loner. It's been hard for me to even think about changing my life, in any way."

"You don't love me, though," she blurted out.

He couldn't pretend to. It would look like a lie. Violet was perceptive. His fingers curled around hers. "Friendship and affection can lead to it," he said gently. "I can't give you any guarantees about happily ever after. But I can promise you affection and companionship and respect. The rest will fall into place. I know it will. Give it a chance. Say yes."

She hesitated. It didn't sound genuine. He wasn't pretending undying love, but he wasn't promising much. She could get companionship and affection from a dog or a cat. What she wanted from Blake was much more. What sort of marriage would it be if he didn't love her, as she loved him?

He obviously enjoyed her physically, but everybody said that passion wore itself out eventually. After it was gone, what would Blake have left if he didn't love her as well as want her?

"You're thinking it to death," he accused. "Listen to me. I'm tired of living alone. I'm willing to take a chance if you are. If things don't work out, it's no problem. We'll go our separate ways." He was already thinking ahead; if she turned out not to be pregnant, there was no reason to think he'd have to stay married to her. But he wasn't about to admit that.

"You mean, we'd get a divorce," she said.

He shrugged. "Sometimes things don't work out. I'm not saying I think we wouldn't make it, Violet. I'm offering you a way out, just in case."

"Isn't that sort of like having a fire engine stand by in case there's ever a fire?" she fished.

He chuckled. "No. It's not." He studied her warmly. "Come on. Give in. You can have any sort of engagement ring you like, and I'll even let you sign an ironclad agreement that you'll never leave me to work for anyone else ever again."

"Why would I sign such an agreement?" she exclaimed.

"For my peace of mind, of course," he told her dryly. "You'd want me to be happy, wouldn't you?"

She lost her apprehension and laughed with him. "That's awful."

"Give me time. I'll get even worse with age," he promised.

"What a horrible thought!"

"I'll promise not to throw dictionaries at you," he added.

"You've never thrown one at me," she recalled. She hesitated. "You didn't throw one at Jessie?"

"It was a thin one," he assured her. "Paperback, and abridged."

She burst out laughing. "No wonder she quit!"

"Oh, that wasn't about the dictionary," he said easily. "That was after I poured coffee over a brief she typed."

She gaped at him, waiting for an explanation.

"It had two spelling errors per line. I wanted to make sure she knew to redo it."

"You couldn't have just asked?"

"Too demeaning," he said. "My way worked much better."

"Your way made her quit!"

"So you could come back," he pointed out. "She wouldn't have quit if I'd just asked her to retype the brief, would she?"

She really liked him. It was surprising how comfortable she felt with him, now, even though he excited her almost beyond bearing. It would be taking a chance, she supposed, to marry him. But she didn't have enough willpower to refuse. Perhaps she could teach him to love her, if she worked at it. At the moment, she felt as if she could do anything. Her heart was soaring with delight.

Her free hand covered his. "I must save other women from you," she said facetiously. "So I suppose I'll have to marry you, after all."

He felt funny in the pit of his stomach. He was willing to marry her out of a sense of duty, although she wouldn't know it. But when she agreed to it, he felt suddenly lighter than air. He felt like the luckiest man alive. That was absurd. He didn't love her. He wanted her. He remembered suddenly the feel of her eager, untried body under his on the living room carpet and his cheeks reflected a ruddy color.

"What is it?" she asked, curious.

"I was remembering my carpet."

It took a minute, but she remembered, too. Her own face flushed.

He laughed softly, wickedly. "At least, in that department we're very compatible, aren't we, Violet," he taunted.

"Devil!" she accused, glancing around to make sure nobody heard him.

"It's okay. We're alone on the planet," he assured her in a mock whisper. "We're invisible to the rest of humanity. That being the case, how do you feel about linoleum?" he asked with a speculative glance toward the floor.

"Blake Kemp!" she exclaimed, smacking him on the arm.

He grinned at her. It was a genuine smile. He'd never felt such pleasure in a woman's company. Well, not since Shannon. The thought of Shannon wiped the smile from his face and left him haunted.

She saw that, and her face fell. "Something's wrong, isn't it?"

He couldn't tell her the truth. "I was thinking about your mother," he lied.

"Oh. Oh, dear!" She bit her lip. "Blake, I can't leave her alone. I wouldn't dare."

"How would you feel about having someone stay with her, around the clock, if we visited her often?" he asked, looking for compromises.

"I don't know…"

"We won't get married in the next two days," he said with a comforting smile. "We've got plenty of time to work something out."

"Yes," she murmured, but she was wondering what he meant about plenty of time. He didn't sound as if he was expecting to marry her soon.

He let go of her hand and reached for his coffee cup. "Don't borrow worries, Violet," he chided gently. "Everything falls into place, given time."

"I suppose so."

"Want dessert?" he asked.

She grimaced. "Not really," she confessed. "It's too hard to work it off once I gain it." Then she remembered that she was going to be gaining a lot of weight, soon, and her spirits drooped. Her hormones were already reflecting her pregnancy. She was going to go through a lot more changes in the near future.

"I like the way you look," he said, his voice deep and soft.

She lifted worried eyes to his. "Do you, honestly?"

He nodded.

She finished her own coffee, just as Jan, the young woman who worked for Barbara, brought Mrs. Hardy's supper in a bag for Violet.

"Should we tell Mama yet?" she asked Blake.

He hesitated. He was still getting used to the idea of having to get married. He didn't want to tell anybody.

"We could wait, a few days, at least," she suggested.

"Do you want to?" he replied, surprised.

"Yes," she said firmly. "I need time to get used to the idea myself," she confessed with a shy smile. She didn't add that she didn't think he was serious about getting married, and she didn't want her mother to be disappointed in case he found a reason to back out of it. Maybe it had been an impulse, asking her to marry him, and he was already regretting it.

"If that's what you want," he agreed easily.

He walked her to her car. The parking lot was crowded and he wasn't keen to give local citizens any more reason for gossip. He caught her hand and touched it to his lips. "I'll see you in the morning," he said.

"Right. I enjoyed supper," she added with a shy smile.

"So did I. We'll have to spend more time together. I don't know much about you, do I?" he asked gently.

"I don't know a lot about you, either."

"All the more reason." He checked his watch. "I've got to go. I'm expecting a phone call about a case, at home. It's almost time. See you tomorrow."

"Yes." She would have said more, but he was already walking away. He didn't break stride until he reached his car, and he didn't look back.

Violet watched him drive away with an odd sense of foreboding. He didn't act like a newly engaged man. He didn't act like a man eager to marry, either. She got into her car and drove home. She was more determined than ever not to mention their so-called engagement to her mother.

The rest of the week dragged on, with Violet successfully hiding her morning sickness both from her mother and her co-workers, and Blake.

It worried her that Blake didn't announce their engagement, or treat her any differently. She grew depressed, and it showed.

Blake noticed. Friday afternoon, he held Violet back after Mabel and Libby left. He locked the front door, drew her into his office and closed that door, too.

Sometimes, a sacrifice was called for. That was what he told himself when he drew Violet into his arms and bent to kiss her with forced enthusiasm.

But the minute he felt her soft mouth open under his, it stopped being a sacrifice. He lifted her body against his and deepened the kiss. She moaned under his lips. He caught his breath, his arms contracting hungrily. It had been a long, dry spell, and he was reacting badly to it. He felt himself go taut as the kiss moved into deeper, more urgent dimensions.

He bent to lift her, his mind no longer on pretense or fabrication. He had only one thought in his mind, to relieve the need that was drawing his powerful body as tight as a cable.

"Blake, we…shouldn't…" she tried to protest when he laid her out on the sofa and melted down onto her.

His mouth stopped the halfhearted little protest. His hand was busy on fastenings. In seconds, she felt her bare breasts

under his equally bare chest. It was so sweet that she couldn't
even manage a defense.

One lean leg inserted itself between both of hers under her
skirt and he groaned harshly as he dragged her briefs down
and found the fastenings of his slacks.

"I'm sorry," he ground out into her mouth as his hips
moved down and she felt him in growing intimacy. "I'm
sorry, Violet," he groaned, shivering. "I can't hold it…!"

He was genuinely out of control. His body impaled hers
with quick, deft movements that should have been uncomfortable. But she was hungry for him, too. She opened her
legs with a shaken little sigh and arched her hips to encourage him.

Her hands found their way into his thick, wavy hair and
caressed it while he moved on her in intense passion.

In some ways, it was far more exciting than a slow seduction. He was at fever pitch, and she was quickly following
him into the fire. It made her feel oddly protective that he was
that desperate for her. It was honest. No man could have pre-
tended the passion she felt in him.

"Here," he whispered urgently, shifting her leg with one
lean, strong hand. "Lift it over…mine. Hurry. Yes. Yes!"

He pushed down against her, lifting his head so that he
could see her face, her eyes. They were open, dark, almost
shocked. But her body was encouraging him. He felt her lift
to meet each deep, hard thrust. He felt her softness envelop
him, cradle him, in that secret warmth. He was flying. He was
burning alive. His whole body was one long, throbbing ache.

The tension built to insane proportions. He gasped with
every hard thrust, his eyes blazing with desire, his body rigid,
shuddering, with it.

His fingers contracted on her soft thigh, pulling her up to him.
His teeth clenched as he looked into her wide, shocked eyes.

"I've never watched…with anyone else," he managed in a deep, shaken whisper.

She couldn't answer him. She was spiraling up with him into some dark, hot pleasure that built and built with no relief from the tension that strained her muscles and left her shivering with every movement of his lean hips.

"This is insane," he managed harshly.

Her breasts pushed up against his chest, rubbing hard against it while her hands went between them and stroked down to his flat belly.

He groaned harshly and shuddered. "Yes," he choked. "Yes, do that…do it!"

He arched up, feeling the throbbing pleasure like a knife in him. He couldn't think. He could barely breathe. He hoped she was going with him, because he couldn't stop, couldn't stop, couldn't…stop…!

He cried out, his voice hoarse and strained as his body convulsed over hers. She watched him, fascinated, feeling the deep throb inside her as he shivered and stiffened and then, suddenly, collapsed and gasped for breath.

She was still tingling, but he hadn't given her enough time. She felt sad; cheated. She didn't want to say anything. At least he needed her, if nothing more.

He managed to steady his breathing, although he was still fiercely aroused. He lifted his head and looked at her taut, drawn face. She hadn't gone with him. She was still hungry.

He felt a tenderness toward her at that minute that he'd never felt in his life. She wasn't even complaining. She loved him.

Loved him. The thought made him humble. He reached between them and touched her blatantly, his body controlling her when she jerked in protest.

"Oh, no," he whispered softly, his hand moving gently until he found the place, and the pressure, that made her gasp and lift up. "No, I'm not stopping until you go as high as I did, no matter what it takes." He bent and brushed his mouth slowly over her lips. She shivered as his touch became more insistent. "I'd do anything for you," he whispered into her mouth.

"Blake," she moaned, her fingers gripping his shoulders painfully as the pleasure grew.

"Yes, you're ready now," he whispered, lifting his head to look at her. "I'm going to watch you this time. I like the way your eyes go black when I take you over the edge. I like the way your breasts swell under my mouth. I like feeling you shiver, inside, and ripple around me when you feel that exquisite fulfillment."

The words were as exciting as the way he was touching her. But she was far beyond answering him. Her body was lifting rhythmically, pulsing, her eyes fixed on his face as the pleasure grew so tight that she felt as if she might blow apart from the tension.

Her legs drew apart and she sobbed, her nails biting hard into him as the silvery delight suddenly became dark and throbbing and urgent. "Blake, now," she pleaded, gritting her teeth. Her eyes closed on a wave of pleasure. "Now! Please, please, please…!"

He moved, thrusting deep inside her. The single, hard motion was enough to take her right into the sky. She arched up, shuddering again and again as the ecstasy rippled over her in savage waves. She couldn't see him. She felt him in her body as she exploded like a meteorite.

"Yes," he whispered, unbearably excited by her explosive climax. He ground his teeth together and moved harshly on her, driving for his own fulfillment. They strained together in a hot, fierce silence as the pleasure melted their bodies together for one long, aching instant of perfect communion.

She cried when it was over. The other time it hadn't been so intense, so overwhelming. She cried and couldn't stop.

Blake lifted his damp head and looked at her, his body still trembling faintly from the violence of their coming together.

She opened her eyes and looked into his, and saw something she never expected. She saw utter shock.

Nine

Violet struggled to breathe. She was suddenly aware of the closeness of their bodies joined together so intimately that she could even feel the faint pulsation of him inside her.

He propped himself on his forearms, still fighting to get his breath, and looked into Violet's blue eyes. He'd never felt such a primitive urge to possess a woman, not even Shannon. His feelings for her had been tender, protective, almost passive. He'd never wanted to ravish her. But it was different with Violet. He felt an aching, violent hunger for her. It seemed to grow by the day in strength and power.

But even so, there was tenderness. Her body was soft and pliable, and he breathed in her faint perfume with delight. He traced her eyebrows with a long forefinger, his eyes searching over her face, her throat, her swollen breasts. He touched them tenderly. He thought about his child in her womb and shivered. Would she nurse the baby? he wondered, and he felt suddenly the magic and fear of creation. She was carrying his child. His child…

His breath caught. He bent and touched his mouth to her eyes, closing them tenderly. His fingers speared into her thick hair and tilted her face so that he could close his lips over her mouth.

Violet didn't understand. It wasn't like last time. He was different, suddenly.

He lifted his head and smiled at her. "So much for abstaining until the ceremony," he murmured ruefully.

She flushed.

He laughed softly. "Embarrassed?" he teased. "You shouldn't be. This is one of the most important parts of any marriage. I've seen couples who were compatible in every other way end up in divorce court because one couldn't satisfy the other in bed."

"We don't seem to have that problem," she agreed shyly.

He traced her cheek. "You should have told me that you weren't satisfied," he said softly. "I could see it, fortunately for you. But I don't like thinking you'd let me leave when you were still aching for satisfaction."

She studied him curiously. "I thought men were only concerned with their own pleasure."

"Not this man," he replied, his voice deep and soft. He smiled quizzically. "You enjoy me, don't you?" he asked conversationally. "I'm glad. I thought you might have hang-ups because you'd abstained all your life."

"So did I," she confessed with a soft laugh. "I can't think when we're like this."

"I noticed," he replied. "You dive in headfirst and give it everything you've got." He kissed her softly. "I love the way you are with me, Violet," he said seriously. He drew away slowly, aware of her faint embarrassment. He smiled, because he liked that little sign of insecurity. He liked knowing he was her first man.

She fumbled her clothes back into place. When she finished, he was already opening the door.

"Your mother is going to be worried," he said, glancing at the clock. "You should call her before we leave."

She went to the phone and made the call, inventing a few letters that had to be done after hours. Her mother wasn't worried, and sounded amused. Violet gave Blake a wry glance when she hung up.

"She didn't buy it, did she?" he asked, amused.

"She was young, once."

"So she was." He drew her into his arms and held her for a long moment, his expression worried. He'd only just thought about the baby and how rough he'd been. It was a protective impulse that had just started. She was carrying his child…

"I didn't mean to be that rough," he said suddenly. "I just…lost it when I started kissing you," he confessed quietly. "I didn't hurt you, did I?"

"Of course not," she said, and thought immediately of the baby. Would sex hurt her child? Surely not. Lou had said not to lift. She hadn't said anything about sex. It would be all right. Of course it would.

She followed Blake silently to the front of the office and waited while he turned out the lights and locked up.

"Go straight home," he said softly. "I'll follow you to the turnoff."

"You don't have to do that," she said, surprised by his concern.

"I know. Come on."

He helped her into her car and then got into his. She saw him in her rearview mirror until she turned off on the short road that led to the house she shared with her mother. She felt warm and secure until she pulled into her driveway and remembered that he hadn't said one word about seeing her again during the weekend.

He didn't call, either. She drove up to Victoria Saturday to get her prenatal vitamins and spent the weekend making an afghan while she kept her mother company. She'd been sure that Blake would at least phone her. But he didn't.

She felt oddly used by Sunday evening. He'd needed her Friday night. It had been sweet, but completely physical on his side. She could feel that he had no strong emotional bond with her. It was physical, and that wasn't going to last. She wondered why he'd asked her to be engaged to him. He couldn't know she was pregnant.

At least, that's what she thought until Monday morning. Mabel and Libby were hard at work on documents for court. Violet had gone back to Blake's office to carry him a message from a caller, because he was on the other line and she didn't want to interrupt him in what might have been a private conversation.

She hesitated outside the door, which had been left cracked. What she heard caused the written message to fall to the floor. It broke her heart.

"What else could I do?" he was asking someone in a heavy, hunted tone. "Her mother is in seriously bad health and she's already upset about the manner of her husband's death. If she knew that Violet was pregnant out of wedlock, it might kill her. Besides all that, it's a small community and everybody knows us. There's no way Violet would agree to a termination, so marriage is the only possible resolution."

He paused for several seconds before he spoke again, obviously listening to the person on the other end of the line. "I know," he said, and sounded worn. "I know. But she won't find out. I'll never tell her. I can give her enough to make her happy. She and her mother will never want for anything. After the child is born, we'll make whatever decisions have to be made. I'll make sure she's taken care of, whether or not the marriage continues. Yes. Yes, I know."

Violet bent to pick up the fallen piece of paper. His voice droned on. Whoever he was talking to seemed long-winded.

She turned and went back down the hall to the waiting room. She wasn't thinking clearly at all. It was impossible to make any rational decision until she could sort out her priorities.

She sat down at the computer and put the phone call memo on top of a stack of papers beside the printer tray. She felt numb for the moment. That was good, because she was going to have hysterics when she could reason again.

The front door opened and Libby came in. She glanced at Violet and hesitated.

"Are you okay?" she asked at once. "You're white as a sheet!"

Violet swallowed hard and then swallowed again. "I feel a bit woozy," she confessed, feeling her forehead. "There's some sort of bug going around. I'll bet I've caught it."

"Can I get you anything?" Libby asked, concerned.

"What's wrong?" Blake asked, coming into the room, frowning.

"Violet's feeling ill," Libby said. "Maybe you should go home," she told her co-worker.

"Not a bad idea," Blake agreed. "Do you want me to drive you?" he added.

"I can drive," Violet managed in a husky, soft tone. She didn't meet his eyes. "I'm just a little sick. It's nothing. Really."

Blake helped her up and walked outside with her. "Call me when you get home," he said firmly. He hesitated. "On second thought, I think I should go with you."

"No, there's no need for that," she said at once. "I'm fine," she repeated. "I just need to lie down."

He looked uncertain, and he frowned. "You look pale."

She had a good reason to look pale, but she couldn't tell him what it was. "I'll be fine tomorrow," she replied.

"Violet…" he began softly.

"See you tomorrow, boss man," she interrupted with a faint smile, and walked away.

Blake watched her go with odd twinges of guilt. If he'd been a proper fiancé, he'd have picked her up and carried her to his own car and driven her home. He'd have stayed with her, too. He didn't understand his own nebulous feelings. He'd spent a miserable weekend trying to resolve them. The futility of his situation had made him moody. He resented the knowledge that Violet was pregnant. He resented the trapped feeling he'd had all weekend, which had kept him from phoning her, despite their passionate interlude in the office. The baby was as much his fault as hers, of course, but he wasn't facing facts well. He was being selfish. It was just that his whole life had turned upside down. He was uneasy about being a husband, much less a father. He'd been alone for so long. But that was no reason to let Violet suffer for something that was his own fault. She was sick, and it was his responsibility to take care of her now.

Resolutely, he turned and started toward her car, but it was only in time to see her drive out of the parking lot. She was gone in a heartbeat and he felt like the world's biggest louse. She was sick and he was letting her go home alone.

While he was debating his next step, and reaching into his pocket for his car keys, Libby stepped to the door to tell him he was wanted urgently on the phone. One of his clients had been arrested.

He went back inside, fate having decided the next move for him.

* * *

Violet cried all the way home. She'd hoped that Blake really cared about her, that he wanted her for keeps, that he'd be thrilled when he learned about the baby. But he already knew, God knew how, and he wasn't thrilled. He was only marrying her for appearances. He felt trapped. He didn't want Violet in any way at all, except perhaps physically. It was a harsh blow.

She stayed in her car until the tears stopped and she was able to act with some sort of normalcy. She checked her eyes in the mirror to make sure they weren't red. She didn't want to alarm her mother. About one thing Blake was right: her mother would be horrified if she knew about the baby.

With a forced smile, she called to her mother as she walked in. Mrs. Hardy looked up from her soap opera and waved and smiled absently, going right back to the action on the screen.

It was a reprieve. Violet went into her bedroom and changed into loose jeans and a sweatshirt. She did lay down for a few minutes, certain that her mother wouldn't be moved by a hurricane until her program went off.

She had to make a decision, and quickly. She couldn't hop on a bus and leave town. It would be impossible to move her mother right now, and not only because of the impending legal problems if Janet Collins was ever found and prosecuted for the death of Violet's father. She couldn't leave because her mother wouldn't survive being uprooted. She loved Jacobsville.

That being the case, temporarily Violet had only one possible course of action. She had to get out of Blake's office. She was uneasy about calling Duke Wright back and going to work for him again, but she didn't have a list of potential employers. She wouldn't be able to hide her pregnancy for a long time, but for several weeks at least she wouldn't show. That gave her a little time to make decisions.

She picked up the phone and called her former boss.

Minutes later, she walked into the living room. The credits were rolling on Mrs. Hardy's soap opera, and the elderly lady was drying her eyes.

"It was so sad," she told Violet. "Harry had loved Eunice for years and years, and just when he asked her to marry him, he died of a heart attack."

"Yes, that's sad, all right." She bent and kissed her mother gently. "How are you feeling?"

"I should be asking you that, dear," she replied with a pointed stare. "You look very pale. Are you all right?"

"I think I've picked up a bug," Violet told her. "I came home early. It was okay with the boss man," she added with a forced smile. "I'm going to fix something nice for supper."

"If you like," Mrs. Hardy said, but she looked worried.

Violet wasn't about to tell her the rest, that she'd just agreed to go back to work for Duke Wright. Her former employer hadn't been able to replace her, and he was overjoyed that she was willing to come back.

The only bad thing was that she'd agreed to be in his office Monday. Now she had to tell Blake Kemp that she was leaving again, and why. It made her sick at her stomach even to contemplate it.

Blake phoned her as soon as he'd pacified his worried client, but Mrs. Hardy answered the phone and said she was sorry, but Violet had gone to bed with a headache. He hung up and went home. But he didn't sleep.

All night long, his selfishness haunted him. Violet was sweet and kind, and she loved him. He could look for the rest of his life and never find a woman half as honest as she was.

Ever since she'd come to work for him, she'd nurtured him, cared for him, to the extent that his heart lifted just at the sight of her in his office. Since they'd become intimate, his body ached for her night and day. He knew that he was her first man, that she wanted no one else. And now she was carrying his child under her heart. After all that, he'd proposed to her only because he felt an obligation, not because he wanted her or his child.

Now, with his mind finally functioning again, he realized what a lucky man he was. Why had it taken him so long to know it?

He got up before dawn and made himself a big breakfast. He was going to the most exclusive jewelry store in Jacobsville and he was going to buy Violet a diamond so big that it would blind her. Perhaps he'd felt trapped into proposing before, but he was only beginning to see what a wise thing he'd done. He was going to make Violet believe that she was the luckiest woman on earth. He'd bring her flowers, take her to the theater, buy her presents. He laughed at his own lightheartedness. He'd never felt so happy.

Violet sat down at her desk, somber and quiet on the following Monday morning. Her demeanor made her co-workers nervous. Especially when she started cleaning out her desk.

Blake walked in the door, smiling.

Violet looked up at him with an expression he couldn't comprehend.

"What are you doing?" he asked suddenly, when he realized she was putting her things into a cardboard box.

"I'm going back to work for Duke Wright," she said quietly.

He stood completely still, his mind not working at all as he stared at her, uncomprehending. "You're quitting, again?" he exclaimed.

She glared at him. "Yes, I'm quitting!"

Mabel and Libby exchanged glances and rose at the same time from their desks. "We're going over to the bakery for bear claws!" they announced, and ran for it.

"You just came back to work here!" Blake burst out, barely noticing the front door close behind the two women.

"And I'm just leaving!" she said, slamming down a stapler on the desk.

"Why?"

"Why?" she exclaimed. "How can you ask me that? You're only marrying me because you know about the baby!"

His indrawn breath was all the confirmation she needed.

"Yes," she said coldly, her anguish in her blue eyes as she looked up at him. "I know, Blake. I heard you talking on the phone."

Talking on the phone. Talking... His mouth opened as he met her sad eyes. Dusky color tinted his high cheekbones and his teeth clenched. Damn fate for letting her overhear that indelicate conversation with Dr. Lou Coltrain. Why, why, hadn't he closed the door?

Violet felt her last hope fly away as she saw his guilty expression. He had meant what he said, she thought. He was only marrying her to give their child a name and keep her mother from having a fatal stroke from the shame.

"A lot of marriages start with less than we have," he said after a minute, choosing his words carefully.

"But we'd have been starting without what matters most, Blake," she told him. "Love."

He almost blurted out that she loved him and he knew it. But that would put the last nail in his coffin. He didn't dare say it.

He drew in a long breath. "I won't try to stop you," he said quietly. "If this is what you really want. But I wish you'd reconsider."

She shook her head. "I don't want to stay here with you feeling sorry for me and everybody speculating on why."

"If you leave, you'll hear plenty of speculating," he replied with visible impatience.

She turned back to her desk, feeling empty inside. "I can't stay."

"Well, don't expect me to try to stop you," he replied furiously. "If you'd rather go out there and tell the whole planet that you're pregnant and you won't marry the father of your child, be my guest!"

"And that lovely sentiment is exactly why I'm leaving!" she raged. "You aren't concerned about me, you're concerned about what people think! Your reputation might be ruined, isn't that it? You might lose clients!"

His eyes blazed at her. "What about your mother, Violet?" he shot back, seeing the point hit home as she winced. "How is she going to feel when she finds out?"

She bit her lip. "Mama will understand."

"Think so?" he replied sarcastically. "How about Duke Wright?"

"Excuse me?"

"When you start showing, what is he going to think? And his employees, not to mention his ex-wife!" He glowered at her numb expression. "They'll think it's his!"

She gasped. "They…won't!"

"Bull!"

She glared at him. It was just too much, all at once. She didn't want to believe what he was saying, but it was the truth. Her face grew redder by the minute.

He glared right back. His eyes narrowed on her thickening waist. His expression changed. He'd never thought of children. At least, not since Shannon's death. Now, he began to wonder what a child of his might look like. Would it have dark hair like his and Violet's? Would it have blue eyes? Would it be a boy, or a little girl?

"You look…odd," she commented.

"I was thinking about the baby," he said absently, his eyes still on her waist. "I never really thought about being a father. I've been alone most of my adult life."

"So have I," Violet confessed.

"What do you want?" he asked, meeting her eyes levelly.

She blinked. "I...haven't thought about that. Not much anyway."

He moved a step closer. "What would you like to have?"

She was lost in his eyes. "Little girls are nice," she ventured. "I like to knit and crochet and quilt. I could...teach her."

His breath caught. A little girl. He thought about Rey Hart's little girl. The family had come to see him about a minor legal matter and Celina came with them. She was barely six months old, dark-haired and fascinating to Blake. He'd watched her like a hawk, noting that Rey was a pushover for his daughter, to his wife Meredith's amusement. The same could be true of Judd Dunn and Christabel's twins. Everyone in town was indulgently amused at how easily a tough guy like Judd Dunn was reduced to putty when he held those babies.

"Little girls are nice," he agreed softly.

"But I wouldn't mind a boy, either. I like baseball and soccer," she continued. "I can still bat and catch and kick."

He smiled. "So can I."

Her face fell as reality came rushing back. "You don't really want a child, Blake," she said sadly. "You're doing the right thing, offering to marry me. But it wouldn't work."

"You don't know that," he said. "A lot of couples start out with less than we have. I said some stupid things on the phone, and you heard them. But I'm still in the early stages of this. You've had time to think about the baby. I haven't." He stuck his hands in his trouser pockets. "I don't react well to change," he said flatly. "I have to have time to work through what it's going to mean."

Violet sighed worriedly. "Yes, but you'd feel trapped."

He shrugged. "Honestly, maybe I do, a little," he confessed. "But that's temporary. I just need a little time, Violet."

"I know that. So do I." She turned and went back to her desk, to the box she was packing up. "Duke's willing to let me come back. I'm going. In a few weeks, when you know what you want, we can talk."

"In a few weeks, you'll be showing, Violet," he replied shortly.

She turned. "I'm plump," she said without heat. "I won't show for a while."

"Plump." He smiled gently. "Womanly is a better adjective. You look lovely."

Her eyebrows arched.

"I'm not trying to win you over," he said when he saw her expression. "I actually mean it. There are a lot of things about you that I like. Besides, the cats like you."

"Does that win me points?" she ventured.

He chuckled. "They don't like many people. And they attacked a pizza delivery guy one night, one cat climbing up each leg. I have to pay extra now to get him to come back. And I have to promise to lock up Mee and Yow before he pulls into the driveway."

"Ouch."

"It could have been the anchovies, I guess," he said in hindsight. He eyed her quietly. "All right, if you're determined to leave again, I won't stand in the way. But you have to do some thinking yourself. The person we both need to consider is the baby. He, or she, has no choice at all about this."

She grimaced. "I didn't think about…precautions."

He smiled slowly. "We were both a little preoccupied. Both times."

She flushed.

He laughed. "It was very good. I imagine I could search for the rest of my life and never find a woman who suited me so well, physically."

She shrugged. "I thought men could find pleasure with anybody."

"So they say. But I've stopped looking."

The way he was looking at her made her toes curl in her shoes. He seemed to be genuine about his feelings. But he didn't love her. And she did love him. It would be a poor match.

"I plan to call you, often," he said. "I'm giving advance notice. Don't think because I'm agreeing to let you leave, that it means I'm giving up on you. I'm not."

Her eyes widened. "Oh."

"And I'd prefer it if you didn't tell your mother we're having problems," he added. "She doesn't need any more upsets."

"Yes, I know. I won't tell her," she agreed, her head bent over the box.

"There's a rumor that Duke's wife may be coming down with their son, for a quick visit," he added. "It may be for legal reasons, but I think she's heard about the new lady vet who's working for Wright."

Her eyes twinkled. "Jealousy?"

"Who knows? But it would be nice if they could patch up their differences. A child needs two parents," he added firmly, and he wasn't talking just about the Wrights, Violet guessed.

"Yes. A child does need two," she agreed.

He moved forward and picked up the box for her. His eyes were solemn. "I should have gone with you, the afternoon you left sick," he said unexpectedly. "I was going after you when the phone rang and I had to placate a frightened client."

"You were?" she exclaimed, surprised.

"I was. Open the door."

She did, and he followed her through to the outside.

She eased her mother past the fact that she was going back to work for Duke Wright with a simple explanation—she and Blake weren't getting much work done staring at each other, so she was solving their problem until they got married and settled down.

Her mother gave her an odd look, but she smiled and let it go.

True to his word, Blake called Violet every day. She was shy at first, but he related the day's happenings and the office gossip, and after a couple of days, it was very nice to have someone to talk to who knew everything that was going on around town.

But then Janet Collins was arrested in San Antonio and charged with the murder of Violet's father.

As he had when the autopsy results on Mr. Hardy came in, Blake didn't phone Violet. He went to Duke Wright's house and delivered the news in person.

Violet's expression wasn't easily read. "What now?" she asked slowly, her hands poised over the keyboard of the computer.

"Now she gets formally charged with first degree murder. She'll be arraigned next Monday in San Antonio."

"Should Mother and I go, do you think?" she wondered, hoping not. It would be an ordeal to have to see the woman who'd killed her father.

"That's not necessary," he replied. "Although your mother will probably have to testify at the trial in order for us to get a conviction."

"What good will that do?" Violet asked miserably. "It

will only upset her. She never saw Janet with my father, anyway."

Blake held up a hand. "I'm afraid she did," he replied, watching her expression turn from worry to shock. "She never told you, but she walked in on them in the motel, just before your father collapsed and was taken to the hospital."

"That's where police got the trace evidence that linked her to poison," Violet recalled, still battling shock about her mother's secrecy all these years.

"Yes, and it was fortunate for us that your mother did walk in on them, because she's not only an eyewitness, but her very presence shocked Janet into running for her life. In the process, she left behind the glass the poison was in. Her fingerprints are on it," he added, "although nobody knows that except the crime lab, the police, and me. And now you," he amended. "There's more than enough evidence to convict her of murder. Your mother will provide the motive and eyewitness identification that links Janet to the motel room, your father, his bank account and her penniless state. They'll try to introduce evidence from the previous poisoning of a patient in a nursing home who left her his estate. The old man's son is more than willing to testify."

"You've been busy," she exclaimed, when she realized that he'd been investigating the status of the case against Libby.

"I have, indeed." He slid his lean hands into his slacks pockets, smiling slowly at Violet in a way that made her toes curl up in her shoes.

Harley Fowler walked in with Duke Wright, talking about a bull Harley's boss, Cy Parks, had bought and sent Harley to transport, when they spotted Blake.

Duke's big fists curled at his sides. "What are you doing in my house?" he demanded of Blake.

Blake glanced at him with a rueful smile. "Just talking to

the mother of my child," he said, dropping the bombshell.
Just as well, he was thinking, to get two birds with one stone,
especially since both men were temporarily single. No way
was one of them going to mess around with his Violet.

Ten

But if Blake was feeling smug, Violet was trying to rein in a totally different emotion. She glanced from Harley's amused expression to Duke's shocked one, back to Blake's arrogance.

"How dare you!" she raged at Blake, pushing to her feet.

It was a mistake. She was already weak from the effects of pregnancy and lack of sleep. She started to fall.

Blake moved like greased lightning to catch her as she slumped. He hefted her in his arms and cradled her close, smiling. "It's still the first trimester," he told her gently. "You have to watch making sudden moves like that. You could fall."

She glared at him, furious and with no way to retaliate.

Duke's threatening stance had relaxed. He looked at Blake with conflicting emotions. "It's your baby?" he asked slowly.

Blake gave him a look that could have started a brushfire. "How dare you!" he repeated Violet's own earlier statement, and managed to look indignant as well as angry. "What sort of woman do you think she is?"

Duke cleared his throat. "Sorry."

Violet was trying not to smile. It really wasn't funny. But Blake's defense of her made her feel warm all over.

Blake relaxed a little, but he wasn't putting Violet down. "You have to make sure she gets frequent breaks," he told Duke. "So that she doesn't get too tired. I'll come by at lunchtime every day and take her out to a nice restaurant where she can get plenty of protein." He looked thoughtful. "Nothing with hormones or antibiotics, of course, we have to think of the baby."

"Blake!" Violet gasped, hitting his shoulder.

"And she positively can't work late," Blake added belligerently.

Duke was smiling now, and trying to hide it. "Okay," he said agreeably.

Harley was shell-shocked. He'd really liked Violet. But the way Blake Kemp was looking at her made his feelings almost tangible. And she was pregnant. Harley sighed wistfully. He didn't have a lot of luck getting women, despite his history for helping crack a major drug ring in the area.

Blake looked back down at Violet. "Feel okay now?" he asked softly, and smiled at her.

She wanted to curl into his strong body and kiss him until she stopped aching. That would never do, of course. "I'm much better," she said primly, and shifted to let him know that she wanted to be put down.

He eased her onto her feet. "We have to tell your mother."

"About the baby?" Duke wondered aloud.

"About Janet Collins being arrested in San Antonio," Blake corrected. "She's being charged with first degree murder in the death of Violet's father."

Duke and Harley both let out a whistle. "I'm sorry, Violet," Duke said gently. "If you need to leave early, you can. I'll get a temp out here to fill in for you."

"No, it's better if I don't upset Mama by altering my routine," Violet said. "I'll do it when I get off work."

"I'll go with you," Blake said easily.

She met his eyes and it was like lightning striking. She cleared her throat. "Thanks."

He nodded, lost in that soft, hungry gaze.

Duke whacked Harley with a big fist. "Speaking of routines, we've got cattle to move." He glanced at Blake. "I didn't realize why you were here. Sorry about the reception."

Blake shrugged. "No harm done."

Duke hesitated. "I'll make sure she gets enough breaks," he added. "I remember how my wife was, before our son was born." His face closed up.

"We heard she's coming down for a visit," Blake said, fishing.

Duke's poker face was hard to read. "We're discussing a revision of the custody rights. She's spending a lot of time in the air, and the boy stays in a day care center or with a sitter most of the week." His eyes flashed angrily. "I want to bring him here to live."

"Will she do it, do you think?" Violet asked gently.

"It was a messy divorce," he replied. "But I'm just beginning to realize how much of it was my own fault. I ran her off." He shrugged. "Maybe we can work things out better now." He stared at Blake. "You tried to tell me that, and I punched you."

Blake chuckled. "No harm done. I punched back."

Duke managed a smile. "He was a captain in the special forces, did you know?" he asked Violet. "He and Cag Hart served together."

"I don't talk about that," Blake said curtly.

"Well, excuse me," Duke said easily. "It wasn't as if you hid in a foxhole and looked for ways out of combat, you know."

Violet was looking at Blake curiously.

Duke grinned. "He'll tell you one day, I suppose," he said. "Or show you the medals, if he's in a good mood."

Blake's eyes were blazing.

"I'm going!" Duke said, palms out. "Come on, Harley, we'll go load up that bull your boss wants."

"Yes, sir," Harley replied, with a wink at Violet. Blake glared at him. He held his palms out, too, chuckling, and followed Duke out the door.

Violet stared after them, then at Blake. He didn't look guilty. He looked smug, standing there with a grin on his face and his hands in his pockets. He wasn't a man who smiled often. He seemed to do it a lot with Violet, she noticed. It eased her embarrassment.

"Now you'll marry me, won't you?" he mused with pursed lips.

Her eyes narrowed as she sat back down. "That wasn't fair."

His eyes twinkled. "Neither is walking around town with my baby under your heart, smiling at other men. Especially Harley Fowler," he added, just to make it clear.

She blinked. "I'm not interested in Harley, that way."

"Well, he's interested in you. Or he was."

"You're not serious."

"I am." The smile faded as he looked at her, and felt a new and tender protectiveness for her. "You don't have much of a self-image. I've been a bad influence on you, and I haven't given you the support you need. That's going to change."

"Do you feel all right?" she asked warily.

"Maybe Duke isn't the only one who'd done some soul-searching lately," he replied. "I spent weeks putting you down, when you came to work for me. You'd never given me anything except concern and kindness. I resented it. I suppose I knew even that long ago that you were under my skin. I fought it, of course."

"It might just be the baby," she began.

"It might not."

She smiled at him, her eyes softening. "Well, well."

He smiled back. "I'll come by when you get off work and follow you home. We'll both break the news to Mrs. Hardy."

"Mama's tough," she told him. "She seems very frail, but she's got grit."

"So have you. I'm afraid you'll need it, too, when this case goes to trial. It will bring back some painful memories for both of you."

"We faced all that when Daddy died," she said sadly. "Including the loss of his money and our home. At least we'll get some satisfaction at seeing her brought to account for killing him. I hope she'll go to jail."

"So do I, but you can't second-guess a jury. We'll have to supply the prosecutor with as much ammunition as we can get," he added. "I don't want her to slip out of this."

"Neither do I," Violet agreed. She smiled at him. "Thanks."

"I'll see you at five." He winked before he went out the door. Violet sat staring after him, sighing, until she realized that she had work to get done.

Mrs. Hardy knew something was wrong when she heard two cars pull up in the driveway, and especially when she saw Blake and Violet come in together looking somber.

She sat up straight in her chair and folded her hands on her lap. "Okay. What's going on?"

They both started.

"Two cars? Both of you here just after work? It's something big."

"Well…" Violet began.

Blake moved closer. "They caught Janet Collins. She's in jail in San Antonio."

"Hallelujah!" Mrs. Hardy burst out, grinning.

Blake and Violet exchanged puzzled stares.

"Am I supposed to faint or something?" Mrs. Hardy asked. "Sorry. I'm very happy they got her, and I'll be more than happy to testify to everything I know."

"It will be stressful," Violet began, sitting down on the sofa across from her mother.

"Letting her get away with it would be more stressful." She looked at Blake solemnly. "And speaking of stress, when are you two getting married?"

Blake's lips fell open.

"It had better be soon," she added firmly. "I do not want my daughter waddling down the aisle in maternity clothes."

"Mama!" Violet exclaimed, horrified.

"She thinks I'm deaf," Mrs. Hardy told Blake. "I'd have to be, not to hear her throwing up every morning." She studied him belligerently. "Well?"

Blake actually laughed. "I just told her new boss about the baby."

"It will be a scandal," Mrs. Hardy wailed.

"It will be a baby," Blake corrected, smiling tenderly at Violet. "With two parents who'll love and want him very much."

"Indeed they will," Violet agreed, smiling back at him.

"So?" Mrs. Hardy persisted. "When?"

"I suppose if we hurry, we can manage next week," Blake said. "Under the circumstances, the sooner the better. But it won't be a big wedding. I've got cases I can't postpone, so there won't be time for a honeymoon just yet."

"Never mind the honeymoon, you have to legalize my grandchild," Mrs. Hardy continued.

"I'll get right to the arrangements," Blake said. "She can go shopping for a dress and I'll arrange the flowers and the reception."

"What about the minister?" Mrs. Hardy asked.

"We could have a civil service," Violet began, worried.

"We will not," Blake interrupted. "We're having a church wedding. Violet," he continued softly when he saw her face, "it's not as if we're being forced into it." He glanced at Mrs. Hardy and cleared his throat. "Well, we're sort of being forced into it, and we did jump the gun. But we're going to have a good marriage, and it needs a good foundation."

"I'd be self-conscious in church," she murmured.

"Even the Puritans crossed the line when they were engaged," Blake said. "God doesn't expect people to be perfect. Luckily for us all."

"I suppose so," Violet replied.

"People will talk," Mrs. Hardy murmured unhappily.

"They're already talking, and smiling, and laughing," Blake told her with a grin. "It's an open secret all over town. The only thing they're curious about is where we're being married."

"I suppose that's the beauty of small towns," Violet agreed, smiling back. "There are no real secrets. We're all family."

"Exactly," Blake replied. "Now to the next important issue." He watched their faces grow attentive. "Who wants Chinese take-out?" he asked, chuckling.

He went to get the order and brought it back to Mrs. Hardy's. She and Violet already had the places set at the table and they were all hungry. They talked over the potential case against Janet Collins, and the forthcoming wedding. By the time Blake was ready to leave, Mrs. Hardy was smiling and seemed to have no more misgivings.

Violet walked him out to his car, noticing how bright and

clear the night sky was. The stars were brilliant. All around there was the fragrance of the old-fashioned roses Mrs. Hardy grew in her small garden.

Mrs. Hardy had already announced her opinion of living with the newlyweds—and especially Blake's delinquent Siamese. She said she'd prefer torture. So they'd compromised on having a nurse-companion stay with her. Blake would call an agency and have them send over people for Mrs. Hardy's approval.

"She'll be much happier here, I know," Violet told him on the porch. "She loves puttering in her roses. We can visit her a lot."

"We'll come over often and bring supper, too," he said. "She'll have someone qualified to look after her, so you don't have to worry about that." He looked at her curiously. "See how easily things work out, when they're meant to happen?"

She nodded. She moved a step closer to him. It was chilly, despite the usually warm spring nights. She looked up at him quietly. "You won't end up resenting the baby because it forced us into marriage?"

He caught her by the waist and pulled her close. "If I didn't care about you, I'd make provisions for you and the baby and we wouldn't get married," he said surprisingly. "I don't like the idea of divorce. It's messy and it leaves a trail of sorrow behind it. You and I have a lot in common. We're basically the same sort of people. We have the same attitudes. We both love children and animals. There's enough there to start with, and a physical compatibility that I never expected in a million years. I want to marry you. The baby is going to be a bonus."

Tears stung her eyes. "You've thought about this a lot."

"I have. That's why I'm sorry you overheard me talking to Dr. Lou Coltrain," he added, identifying his confidant for the first time. "I wasn't choosing my words, and I was confused. I'm not anymore."

"You're sure about that?" she asked gently.

He nodded. He traced a line down her soft cheek. "I've been alone for a long time. I'm tired of it. I'll adjust, and so will you."

She nodded, but she still looked worried.

"What now?" he asked.

"I'm scared."

"Of getting married?" he asked with a quizzical smile.

"Of the baby," she replied. "They don't come with instruction manuals. They're so tiny, and so fragile…"

He drew her close, laughing softly. "Everybody's afraid of being parents," he said easily. "But babies are tougher than they seem, and there's always Dr. Lou. She's had lots of experience with pregnant people, and she knows a very good obstetrician."

"So I heard."

"Stop worrying," he told her. "We're in this together."

"I suppose we are, at that," she conceded. "We'll have company, too—well, about marriage. Libby and Jordan Powell are getting married."

He grinned. "That's no surprise. He's been in and out of the office several times trying to get her to forgive him."

"Serves him right that she took her time about it," she pointed out. "He and Julie Merrill were a venomous pair. Will Julie go to prison for that arson charge, do you think?"

"She'll probably try to let her employee swing in her place. Don't worry. Chief Grier has another pending charge, one that she won't escape so easily."

"Are you going to tell me what it is?" she fished.

He chuckled. "Not now." He bent and kissed her gently, tugging her close into his arms. They were warm and safe against the chill of the evening. She sighed and kissed him back. His mouth felt as warm as his arms. He was perfect to her.

"Go back in," he said after a minute, running his lean hands over her arms. "You're freezing out here."

"It's supposed to be spring already," she pointed out, shivering.

"If you don't like the weather, wait five minutes," he repeated the standing local joke.

"I believe that." She smiled. "Are we really getting married next week, or was that just to placate Mama?"

"It was to placate me, too," he replied somberly. "I don't want people making snide remarks about you, the way they're talking about Tippy Moore moving in with Chief Grier."

"She was badly hurt," she stated. "Nobody sane is going to think anything of it. Besides, Mrs. Jewell is staying there around the clock. So is Tippy's little brother. There are too many chaperones for much to go on."

"Still, there's talk," he countered. "And they'll have more ammunition with you than they did with Tippy, even considering her miscarriage. It won't take long for someone to notice that you had prenatal vitamins filled up in Victoria."

She gasped. "How did you know that?"

"Lou told me," he said simply, and he smiled. "Well, I am a concerned party," he reminded her. "It's my baby, too." He hesitated, frowning as he looked down at Violet and then at her flat stomach. He felt…odd. He'd never thought about children, except once, long ago, with Shannon. Since then, since the fatal poisoning that had claimed her and her unborn child, he'd been belligerent about not wanting children. But now…

"You're upset," Violet said softly, moving a step closer. "What is it?"

He looked worried. "You know that I've been adamant about never wanting children. I'm not sure you know why."

She'd forgotten that, and it made her heart sink. She knew

he was making the most of a bad situation, but she hadn't wanted to remember how he felt about children. "Some men just don't like them," she began.

He put his forefinger over her mouth. "Shannon was pregnant when she died," he said bluntly. "It was my child."

She didn't look shocked, as he'd expected. He frowned.

"Small towns," she explained softly. "Everybody knows everything."

"You knew that?"

She nodded. "I'm sorry it happened that way."

He drew in a long breath. "Yes. So am I. It was a blow that I never quite got over. Every time I saw Julie Merrill, it brought it all back. She killed another human being for no more reason than she wanted to be class president. She didn't even seem to be bothered by it."

"There are people who feel nothing at all," she replied. "I don't understand it, either. But someday, she'll pay for the evil she's done."

"The sooner, the better," he replied.

She reached up and touched his cheek. "Did you know, about the baby?"

His face went taut. "No. I'm not sure she was comfortable telling me about it. I was more adamant in those days about families than I am now, and that's saying something. That made the guilt worse. I wondered if she'd been tormented, thinking I wouldn't want the child. As it is," he added heavily, "it's a moot point. The baby died with her."

"Did Julie know?" she wondered.

"I never asked. It would make no difference now. But I'd still love to see her lining up for payback, for the things she's done. She shouldn't be allowed to get away with it."

"People don't get away with things, Blake," she said, sounding much more mature than she was as she looked up at him. "It may take years, even a lifetime. But eventually people who hurt other people get it back, doubled."

He traced her mouth softly. She made him feel comforted, safe, secure. He was a tough ex-special forces captain and he really did have the medals to prove it. But she melted him. He wondered if she had any idea what he felt for her. It was like what he'd felt for Shannon, years ago. Shannon. He saw her face, in the casket, white and still, her happy blue eyes closed forever. He felt sick.

It wasn't Violet's fault, and when he saw her uncertain stare, he felt worse. He bent and kissed her tenderly. He was anguished, but he didn't want her to think she was responsible for it. He was remembering Shannon, as he'd last seen her, when the light had gone out of the world. He had to get out of here, to have time to himself to come to terms with the past. "Get some rest. I'll phone you tomorrow," he told her.

He'd promised lunch, but she could tell that the discussion about Shannon was wounding him. She only smiled. "I'll look forward to it," she said. "Drive carefully."

He nodded absently, turned, and went to his car. He didn't look back as he drove away.

Violet hesitated before she went back into the house. She wasn't really worried. He wasn't lying about their physical compatibility, and he did seem to want their child. But he hadn't completely settled the past. He needed time, and she was going to give it to him. She wanted him desperately. But he had to want her just as much. He had to let go of the memory of Shannon.

Somehow, she knew, he would manage that.

She and her mother had an early night. She dreamed about the baby, and awoke feeling flushed and excited about the prospect of bringing a new little life into the world. She didn't care which sex it was. She only wanted a healthy child.

She wondered how she was going to manage to work and raise a family, or if Blake really wanted her to. She liked her job, but she loved the idea of being with her children while they were small, taking them places, reading to them, being with them. Her mother had given up work to be a stay-at-home mother, and she'd never regretted it. Violet knew that she would feel the same. If Blake had been a common laborer, and she had to work to help make their living, she knew she'd cope. But they were in different circumstances. She wanted to try it.

As she walked into Duke Wright's office the next morning, she noticed that her boss was looking uneasy. He glanced up at her approach, and he didn't smile.

"Did I do something wrong?" she asked uneasily.

He shook his head. "Beka's on her way."

"Excuse me?"

"Beka. My…almost ex-wife. And our son."

"Oh." She put down her purse. "Do you need me to do anything?"

"There isn't much to be done," he replied. He moved away from the desk with his hands in his jeans pockets. "I hope she meant what she said on the phone, that she's willing to consider leaving Trent with me."

"Maybe she did," Violet said, trying to be reassuring.

He shrugged. "It's just that she may change her mind if she finds out I've got Delene working here in the lab," he blurted out.

"Does she know Delene?" Violet wanted to know.

He grimaced. "They only met once, at my college reunion. Delene didn't like her, and it showed. See, Beka had barely graduated high school at the time. It was before she went back to college to get her law degree. Delene was in my graduating class—a science major, at that. She always was brainy."

Violet's eyebrows arched. "Well!"

"If she thinks I'm involved with Delene, she may take Trent right back to New York," he said uncomfortably. "What can I do? I can't very well fire the best biologist I've got!"

"You could have Delene go off on a fact-finding trip to Colorado," she suggested.

He looked at her blankly. "Colorado?"

"Isn't the National Cattleman's Association sponsoring some sort of workshop for artificial insemination experts this week?" she wondered.

He pursed his lips. "Why, so they are! There was a brochure about it in the mail last week, remember?"

"Yes, I do." She checked her watch. "You could get her on a plane by noon, if you hurry."

He chuckled. "Violet, you're a wonder!"

"Just a suggestion, boss."

He sighed. "Now, if she'll just go…!"

"Ask her. But you'd better hurry," she pointed out. "You don't have much time."

"I'll do it right now. Uh, those letters on the desk need answering, but I haven't got a minute to dictate them right now. Just catch up herd records, okay?"

"Okay."

He was gone before she had a chance to even answer him. She sat down, amused, and turned on her computer. It was going to be an interesting day.

Two hours later, she was deep in a spreadsheet program, listing daily weight gain quotas and measurements from the new bull yearling crop, when the door opened and a tall, blond woman walked in with a small boy in a suit in tow.

She stopped short when she saw Violet at the desk. She frowned, and peered at the woman. "Do I know you?" she asked slowly.

"Are you Mrs. Wright?" Violet replied politely, and then grimaced, because she was about to be the ex-Mrs. And that might not be a politically correct way of addressing her. Violet flushed.

"I'm Beka Wright," the other woman replied tersely. She moved forward, with the little boy. "Are you new?"

"Yes, ma'am," Violet agreed. "I've been working for Mr. Wright on and off for just a few weeks."

"On and off?" Beka queried, while the child at her side fidgeted and leaned against her leg in its elegant black slacks above high heels.

"Mr. Kemp fires me periodically," she replied. "Or I quit. But I'll be going back pretty soon, I guess, because we're sort of engaged," she added quickly, before the other woman could get the wrong idea about her presence here. She smiled shyly.

"Blake Kemp is getting married?" Mrs. Wright asked. She felt her forehead. "I must feel worse than I thought. Or maybe I'm hearing things."

"No, it's true," Violet assured her. "We're sort of having a baby."

"A baby. Now I know I need to sit down." Mrs. Wright plopped into the chair in front of the desk and hoisted the little boy onto her lap. "Where's my husb…my ex-husband?" she corrected curtly.

"I think he drove Miss Crane to the airport," she replied, and then could have bitten her tongue out for mentioning it.

"Delena Crane?" Her face tightened. "What's she doing here?" Beka demanded.

"Uh, she's going to a conference in Colorado. She's a biologist." She didn't dare add that she worked for Mr. Wright, too.

Beka relaxed, but just a little. "Does she spend much time here?" she asked suspiciously.

"Not much, no." Violet hoped she wouldn't get in trouble for lying.

"Good. I mean, I wouldn't want my son around her," Beka qualified. "She has an attitude problem. When will Duke be back?" she continued.

Violet looked past her and grimaced. "Any second," she murmured uncomfortably.

Beka turned around. Duke Wright was standing in the doorway, his hat cocked low over one eye, his face as rigid as steel. And he wasn't smiling.

Eleven

Duke moved forward into the room, his expression changing when he saw the blond-headed little boy in his wife's lap.

"Hey, Trent!" he called, grinning.

"Daddy!" Trent struggled away from his mother and made a beeline to the tall man who waited, stooping, with his arms open. The child launched himself into them and hugged the man for all he was worth. "Daddy, I missed you so much!" he wept. "Why didn't you come to see us in New York?"

Duke looked tormented. He wouldn't meet his wife's eyes. He kissed the little boy. "I'm glad you came to see me," he replied, smiling at the child. He looked up, meeting Beka's dark eyes evenly. "Hello, Beka."

"Hello, Duke," she replied, not quite meeting his accusing gaze.

"I'm sure you have a motel room by now, but I'd love it if you'd let Trent stay here," he said quietly. "I have a live-in housekeeper, Mrs. Holmes, who loves children. She's a wonderful cook."

Beka seemed uncomfortable. "I…there aren't…well, there isn't a motel room vacant in Jacobsville…" She looked up at him.

"You're welcome to stay here, too," he replied. "I just didn't think you'd want to," he added bitterly.

"I can stand it if you can," she told him. "Our suitcases are in the car. I'll just go get them," she said, rising.

"I'll have one of the boys bring them in for you," he returned curtly. "If that's all right," he added unexpectedly, and without antagonism.

Her thin eyebrows arched and she looked shocked. "Yes. That would be fine. Thank you."

"You're welcome." He put Trent down and smiled at him. "Want to come with me? I'm going out to the corral to get one of my cowboys. He's working a new filly on a leading rein."

"What's a filly, Daddy?" he asked.

"A filly is a young female horse," he replied. "She's an Appaloosa. She has striped hooves and spots on her back," he added with a grin.

"I thought you sold all the Appaloosas!" Beka exclaimed.

"Not all of them," he replied. His eyes went over her red silk blouse and down the black slacks to her small feet in high heels. "You're welcome to join us. It's pretty dusty out there," he added.

She moved toward him, a little hesitantly. "Clothes can be cleaned," she said. She took Trent's hand. "I'd like to see her."

Duke's eyes softened and he smiled. "She's a beauty."

Beka smiled back, following the man and the boy out the door.

Violet watched them go with hopeful feelings. She knew it had been a messy divorce, because she'd been working with

Blake at the time. Her personal opinion had been that Duke Wright was an overbearing, unreasonable tyrant. She had no sympathy for him at all. A woman who married a man like Duke could expect to be owned like a horse. He never asked anyone else's opinion; he gave his. He threw out orders like a military commander, and the first day Violet met him, she'd have liked to see him upside down in a barrel of dirty water.

But he'd mellowed just recently. It was obvious that he was trying to be polite to his ex-wife, even if it was only to help his case with his son. Delene certainly seemed to like him. She grimaced. When Mrs. Wright found out who the new biologist was, she wasn't going to be smiling. It was going to be an explosion of some magnitude...

Blake had gone home in a black mood. Mee and Yow curled up beside him in bed that night and purred while he brooded. He couldn't get that last vision of Shannon out of his mind, lying so still and beautiful in her white coffin. All the long years, he'd wondered if he could have saved her if he'd just agreed to go to the party with her. She'd asked him to, and he'd wanted to go, because even back then he didn't trust Julie Merrill.

But he'd had a court case the following Monday and he'd wanted time to work on his defense. While he was writing up gambits for his opening argument, Shannon was drinking a drug that worked like poison. He hadn't known a thing about it until early the next morning, when her mother had phoned from the hospital to tell him the news.

He'd gone around in a daze for weeks afterward. He hadn't been able to think, much less work. His reserve unit, like Cag Hart's, had been called up in 1991 when Operation Desert Storm sent soldiers to Kuwait to liberate it from invasion. He'd volunteered without a second thought, not at all concerned that he might die.

He'd waded right in with his company, in the thick of the fighting, a captain in a forward unit. During a memorable fire-fight, he'd propelled a tank into the thick of an enemy position and used it like a battering ram to shut down a machine gun nest that was killing his men. He'd been awarded a Purple Heart, because he'd been wounded in the ensuing firefight, and a Silver Star for gallantry in action. Few people around here knew about it. He didn't talk about his military service. Well, except to Cag Hart, who understood. Cash Grier was rumored to have been in Iraq during the same period, but it was a subject Cash didn't encourage. He was even more reticent than Blake, and that was saying something.

He tossed and turned all night, finally giving in around daylight. He got up and made coffee and toast and brooded at the table. Shannon, the war, all that was in the past. He couldn't go back. For all the wonder he'd felt with her, there had never been the spontaneous rush of passion that he felt when he was with Violet. He and Shannon had loved one another, but with a quieter, less tempestuous love. What he felt with Violet was something else again, a whirlpool of delights that left him breathless even in memory.

He thought about the baby. He wondered if it would look like him or like Violet, if it would be a boy or a girl. He could picture himself with a little girl on his lap, reading her bedtime stories, or with a little boy, showing him the telescope and distant planets, and teaching him about rocks. He loved rocks even more than astronomy. He had samples of crystals and meteorites and fossils and all sorts of minerals. He had a metal detector, and in his spare time he loved wandering around the property with it, looking for metallic meteorites. He'd found several over the years. He'd never told Violet about this odd hobby. He wondered if she liked rocks, too.

He finished his coffee and stretched. The cats sat watching him, puzzled at his change of routine.

"I couldn't sleep. Don't you have bad nights?" he asked them.

They blinked. For all the world, they seemed to be listening. Of course, they seemed to watch television, too. Obviously, his lack of sleep was playing tricks on his mind.

"I'm going to marry Violet," he told them. "And there's going to be a little tiny human being here in a few months. You'll both have to adapt."

They blinked again. But this time they looked at each other and then back at him.

He shook his head. He was doing it again, talking to the cats. Violet and the baby would be good for his mental health. Any day now, he was going to think the cats actually understood him.

He got up and went to the sink. Just as he put his coffee cup and plate under the running water, separate sets of teeth dug into separate ankles.

"Eyoowch!" he burst out, and started cursing.

The two cats moved quickly away, in different directions, with their ears back and their tails as rigid as flags. He rubbed the marks, glaring after them.

"I said, you'll have to adapt and I meant it!" he yelled after them.

They walked faster.

He wasn't going to tell Violet about this, he decided as he doctored the small incisions. She'd have him locked up before the wedding!

When Blake went to pick Violet up at Duke's house for lunch, neither Duke nor his wife and son were around.

"Has she left?" he asked Violet covertly.

She shook her head. "They were stiff and polite at first. Now, they're walking around each other like wrestlers looking for a good hold."

He sighed as he tucked her hand into his and they headed toward his car. "I was afraid it might go like that. People don't really change, you know," he added thoughtfully. "They hide traits that bother potential mates, but bad habits always show up eventually."

She stopped walking and looked up at him with twinkling eyes. "Do tell? And what hideous traits are you hiding from me?"

His own eyes twinkled. He bent down. "I'm a rock fanatic."

Her eyebrows levered up. "You like rock music?"

He shook his head. "I like rocks. Meteorites. Fossils. Crystals. Right now, I'm keen on iron meteorites. I go out looking for them with a metal detector on weekends."

She began to smile. "I've got a box of projectile points in my closet," she said. "I picked them up on my grandfather's farm when I was a little girl. Some are big and some are little. I don't even know much about them, but I treasure them just the same. And I've got quartz crystals of all sorts, from amethyst to rose quartz…!"

He hugged her close, laughing. "Of all the coincidences," he burst out.

She hugged him back. "I can see us now, hiking up a mountain with the baby in a backpack and a metal detector," she chuckled.

He drew away so that he could see her face. "We'll take turns carrying him," he mused. "Or her."

"He feels like a boy," she said. "I don't know why."

He bent and kissed her nose tenderly. "We'll love whatever we get. Maybe he'll like rocks, too. And astronomy."

He took her hand again and led her toward the car. He favored his left leg a little and winced as he moved.

"What's wrong?" she asked immediately. "Did you hurt yourself?"

He paused by the passenger door of his car and studied her. "Don't you want to tell me?" she persisted when he hesitated.

"You might want me locked up when I tell you," he mused.

"Be daring."

He laughed. "I told the cats we were getting married and expecting an addition to the family. They looked at each other, and at me. One got on either side of me and they bit both ankles at once and flounced off in a huff."

She didn't say anything. She gave him an odd look.

He shrugged. "I told you you'd want me locked up."

"Do they like tuna?"

He shook his head. "Salmon. They're crazy for it."

"I know where we can get some fresh salmon," she murmured dryly.

He pursed his lips thoughtfully. "It might just work."

"Let's see!"

"First thing after lunch," he promised, putting her in the car.

Chief Grier was in Barbara's Café when they got there, sitting with a somber Leo Hart. They both looked up when Kemp walked in. Grier motioned to him. He left Violet in line to keep his place and paused by their booth.

"Something's going on, I gather?" he asked.

"Something big," Grier agreed. "Leo's brother Simon got some news about Julie Merrill. Remember the drug lord who tried to set up shop here before I came to work on the force?"

"I do," Blake replied. "He was bad news."

"Well, a female drug lord has replaced him, and we think Julie Merrill is her lieutenant. I've been watching a house out of town on the Victoria road where drug smugglers had a hideout that the DEA busted. There's some new activity. I think Julie's involved, along with some prominent local politicians."

Kemp whistled. "Got her in custody?"

"Chance would be a fine thing," Grier replied. "She made bail and got out, but a couple of days later, she made bush bond." In other words, Blake translated, she skipped town.

"If you need help tracking her down, I know a good P.I."

Grier grinned. "Thanks. But I think my contacts are even better than yours. What I'd like to know from you is something that may be painful," he added, and the smile faded.

"You want to know about Shannon Culbertson," Blake said perceptibly. "Julie put something in her drink and she died. But I could never prove it. I tried, believe me!"

"If you have any notes on the case, I'd appreciate a look at them, if it isn't a confidentiality matter," he added.

"Not at this late date," Blake replied solemnly. "Drop by my office in the morning and I'll have them for you. I'd love nothing better than to see Julie Merrill in stripes."

"That makes two of us," Grier agreed. He glanced at Violet, who was looking at Blake with wide, soft, loving eyes. He grinned. "You've got good taste in women, I might say," he told the other man.

"I do, don't I?" Blake said complacently, smiling at Violet, who blushed.

"I hear she's taking prenatal vitamins," Grier murmured wickedly.

Blake didn't fire from the hip. He actually laughed. "Abundantly," he agreed, "or she goes to sleep in her plate." He glanced from Grier to Leo Hart, who was also grinning. "You can both come to the wedding, if you'd like. We decided on the Methodist church. We're announcing it in the paper. No time for invitations. Mrs. Hardy has loaded her shotgun and made significant threats."

"As if that would matter to you," Leo chuckled.

Blake smiled. "I never thought I'd get married, much less be a parent. But it all seems to be falling into place naturally."

He eyed Grier. "I hear you're already taking Tippy's brother fishing with you."

"He's quite a boy, Rory is," Grier agreed. "I like having him around. I like having her around, too."

"So?" Blake prompted.

Grier just shrugged. "We're waiting for a major complication to resolve itself."

"I heard the kidnapper was still on the loose," Blake told him. "You don't think he'd be crazy enough to show up here in town?"

Grier met his eyes evenly. "Without Tippy, there's no case. Kidnapping is a federal offense. It means hard time. The guy is a professional contract killer. I don't have any illusions about Tippy being safe just because she's in my house. I sleep light these days."

Blake nodded. "I hope it works out."

"It will, one way or another," Grier said grimly.

"What about your cats?" Leo asked curiously.

Blake blinked. "What?"

"We've heard some strange stories from people who visited you at home," Leo replied with a chuckle. "They say most all of them came out running."

"And bleeding," Grier added wickedly.

"A few scratches here and there, that's all."

"Yes, but Violet will be living with them."

"She has some ideas that involve fresh salmon," Blake replied, grinning. "They do take bribes."

"Good luck," Grier said.

"Amen," Leo added.

Blake just smiled and went back to Violet.

He told her on the way out of town about Julie Merrill jumping bail, and about the evidence Grier wanted to see.

She looked at him with soft compassion. "It's hard for you

to look back, isn't it?" she asked gently. "Shannon meant a lot to you."

He nodded solemnly. "She did." His head turned toward her. "But the past is gone, Violet. I've made mistakes, trying to live in it. She was a kind woman. She wouldn't have wanted me to be bitter."

She smiled. "You were just hurt," she said. "It takes a lot of time to get over losing people. I know. I still miss Daddy."

"I miss both of my parents," he said unexpectedly. "My father died when I was little. I took care of my mother all the way through school. She died of a stroke the week after I graduated from law school. Shannon was there, with food and comfort, kindness. I was almost out of my mind with grief already. Then, just a few months later, I lost Shannon, too." He glanced at Violet. "I've been hiding, I suppose."

"It isn't hard to see why." She leaned back against the seat. "Leo looks different."

"He's married," he said, laughing. "He's definitely mellowed. All the Hart boys have. It's just amazing. I'd have bet real money that they'd end up crusty old bachelors."

"They said the same thing about the Tremayne brothers," she pointed out. "And look at them!"

He smiled. "Marc Brannon, Judd Dunn, there are two other bachelors I'd have bet on staying single." He shook his head. "Now Cash Grier's about to fall."

"You think Tippy could settle down in a small town?" she asked, aghast.

"You've seen them together. What do you think?"

She sighed. "I think they're crazy about each other, but neither of them is willing to admit it. She's been through a lot, including the miscarriage. That must have been tough. What if the tabloids find out she's here and start on her again?"

His eyes twinkled. "Oh, I think Cash can handle the press."

"Matt Caldwell certainly did, they say, when a reporter targeted his Leslie some years ago, before they were married."

"This is not a good place for outsiders if they ruffle feelings," Blake reminded her.

"I'm glad. I like living here." She sighed worriedly. "Blake, they won't try to make some big news story out of Janet Collins when her trial comes up, will they? She poisoned Daddy and was suspected in still another murder in a nursing home. There aren't that many women serial killers. What if the press comes in here and starts making snacks out of me and Mama?"

"Not a chance," he promised.

His tone was curious. She glanced up at him. "Do you know something I don't?" she asked slowly.

"Let's just say, I'm working on something," he replied. He stopped at the town's only fish market and parked the car. "Fresh salmon," he said as he turned off the engine with a grin. "Let's hope they take bribes!"

The cats were both sitting in the front window when the car drove up.

"That's odd," Blake remarked. "They never wait for me like that unless it's grocery day."

"Maybe they smell the salmon!" she teased.

He made a face. "Fat chance."

Violet picked up the fish and they both went in the front door together.

"Hi, guys," Violet said, wafting the brown-wrapped fish above their heads. "Hungry?"

They both started yowling, sounding for all the world like crying babies as they stood on their hind legs trying to swat the package out of her hands.

"That has to be a good sign," Violet told him.

"We'll see. Come on, girls," he called to them, leading Violet through the living room and into the spacious kitchen. "I'll get their bowls."

He pulled them out of the dishwasher and settled them on the counter. Violet opened the brown package and split the salmon down the middle. The cats were all but climbing the cabinet.

"Here you go, babies," she said softly, and put the fish down.

They both glanced at her with big blue eyes, but only for a minute. They started eating and growling at the same time, determined that each was going to get her own fair share without having her bowl raided.

Blake and Violet moved away while they ate, watching them. It didn't take long. The cats licked their bowls clean and then started bathing themselves. They ignored the humans completely.

"Ungrateful wretches." Blake laughed. He picked up the bowls and put them in the sink, shaking his head.

But Violet had more confidence than before, and she squatted down next to them on the floor. "Beautiful babies," she said softly, smiling. "I'll make sure you have salmon any time you want it."

They stopped bathing and looked at her with those piercing blue eyes.

"Honest," she added.

Mee called to her, got up, and rubbed against her knees. Yow blinked, hesitated, then moved closer, too, but stopped at one brief head-butt against her thigh.

She looked up at Blake. "It's a start," she said optimistically.

He grinned from ear to ear.

They went together to Libby Collins's wedding. She married Jordan Powell in a beautiful church service, with most of the leading citizens of Jacobsville for witnesses. As her brother Curt led her down the aisle, she glanced at Violet, sitting so close beside Blake Kemp, and grinned. They grinned back.

It was a nice ceremony, brief but poignant, and a reception was held afterwards in Barbara's Café. Tippy and Cash waved to them from across the room. So did the Ballengers. Calhoun was euphoric after having soundly beaten old Senator Merrill for the Democratic nomination for state senate in his district. His wife, Abby, was there, too, clinging to her husband's arm. After three children, all boys, they were still very close. Justin Ballenger attended as well, with his Shelby. Like Calhoun and Abby, they had three sons of their own. Shelby was a direct descendant of Big John Jacobs, who'd founded Jacobsville and Jacobs County.

Violet had felt uncomfortable around all the bigwigs at first, but she learned very quickly that they were just ordinary people, and they didn't put on airs. She liked them. It wasn't going to be hard to fit in here.

But she worried about the case against Janet Collins. There was DNA evidence, of course, but there were ways a good defense attorney could twist the truth. She didn't want the woman to get away with what she'd done to Violet's father.

Blake noticed her distracted expression. "Cheer up," he whispered. "People will think it's a wake instead of a wedding!"

She moved, and smiled up at him, clutching her small cup of punch. "Sorry. I was thinking about Mrs. Collins."

He moved closer, tilting her chin up to his blue gray eyes. "Let me worry about it," he said softly. "I promise you, she's not going to get away with it."

She sighed. "Okay, boss man," she said. She stood on tiptoe and touched her lips to his hard mouth. "Whatever you say."

He smiled, pulling her close to kiss her back, very emphatically. When he drew away he was aware of a faint silence around them.

He looked around and discovered that everyone was watching them instead of the newlyweds.

"Better get a ring on her finger by sundown," Cash Grier whispered as he walked by. "Or you may be the next tabloid centerpiece."

Blake grinned at him. "The wedding's next week," he told the police chief. "You're invited."

"I'll bring my whole department," Cash promised.

Blake's eyebrows arched. "All of it?"

Cash nodded thoughtfully. "And I'll have something very nice planned for your wedding day," he added.

Marc Brannon overheard him and drew his very pregnant wife, Josie, closer. "Run for the border," he advised Blake and Violet. "He was waiting for us at my ranch after our wedding, with half the county law enforcement personnel, and I had to threaten him with a shotgun to get rid of him!"

Grier glared at him. "I did not have half of them." He shifted. "Some people I called refused to come. They didn't want to impose on newlyweds, can you believe that?"

"We're leaving town right after our wedding," Blake promised Violet at once.

Grier really glared then, at Blake and the Brannons. "Hmmmph!" he muttered. "Some people have no sense of humor."

"Some people have no sense of privacy," Marc shot right back.

Grier glanced at Josie and grinned. "Didn't I warn you about him?" he pointed at Marc. "And you didn't listen!"

Josie leaned closer to her husband's tall frame. "Oh, he's not so bad," she said complacently. "In fact, neither are you," she added to Cash, "despite your far-reaching reputation."

"What reputation?" Tippy Moore asked with a soft laugh as she walked to Cash and was gathered against him gently. "He's as pure as the driven snow," she drawled with a mischievous flash of green eyes.

Cash bent and kissed the tip of her nose. "Pest."

She smiled back at him and it was like fireworks. "And I planned to make you beef Stroganoff tonight," she said. "But here you are calling me names…"

"Nice pest," Cash qualified.

She shrugged. "Okay. I guess I can live with that. Good to see you," she added to the others as she let Cash lead her away to the punch. She still had plenty of cuts on her pretty face, and some bruises, and she was a little shaky. But what she'd lived through in New York had gained her a lot of sympathy around Jacobsville. It was pretty much an open secret how Cash felt about her, and vice versa.

"There goes a prospective bride and groom, or I miss my guess," Marc Brannon mused.

"Same here," Blake replied. He curled Violet's fingers into his. "I suppose it's contagious," he added, looking warmly into her eyes.

"What about your cat harem?" Marc asked.

"They take bribes," Violet said before Blake could speak. "Fresh salmon."

"Way to go, Violet," Josie chuckled. "Leave it to a woman to find a way around a difficult situation."

"She'd know," Marc replied, smiling at his wife. "She's just joined the local D.A.'s office as a prosecutor. After the baby comes, that is."

"What do you want?" Blake asked curiously.

"Well, we already have a little boy. I'd love a daughter next. But we'll settle for whatever we get," Josie said warmly, smiling up at her husband, who readily agreed. "I can hardly wait."

Blake looked down at Violet with a softness in his eyes that made her heart float. "Neither can I," he said gently.

Violet blushed scarlet and nuzzled her cheek against his chest.

"We're expecting, too," Blake told the Brannons with a quiet smile. "It's going to be a wonderful year."

"You can say that again," Marc replied. "Congratulations."

"You, too."

Violet closed her eyes as the conversation drifted away. She wondered if she could die of happiness.

Twelve

Violet was nervously waiting in the hall for the organ to sound. Her mother was in the front pew. Half of Jacobsville was seated in the rest of the pews. She noticed that big Cag Hart was acting as best man for her husband-to-be. She had nobody to give her away. But it was something of an archaic custom, she tried to remind herself. She wasn't being given or sold to any man, regardless of how much she loved him.

She plucked nervously at the waistline of her beautiful white satin gown, hoping the slight swell didn't show too much. It wouldn't matter a lot. Most people already knew she was pregnant. She smiled. She and Blake would love their child. She had no more doubts about him, or herself. It would work out.

The organ sounded and she jerked her mind back to the occasion, tightening her grip on her bouquet of baby's breath, white roses, and lily of the valley. She took a deep breath and stepped out on her right foot, just as a big, gentle hand caught her left hand and tucked it into his elbow.

She looked up, startled, into twinkling green eyes.

"I'm not quite old enough to be your father," Cy Parks said in a loud whisper, "but Blake said you wouldn't mind."

She grinned up at him. "I won't mind at all, Mr. Parks. Thank you!"

"That's okay. You can do the same for me one day," he said, tongue-in-cheek.

She started giggling and only stopped when "The Wedding March" was belted out on the piano.

"Straight faces, now," Cy murmured.

"You bet!" she agreed.

They walked down the aisle, to where Blake was waiting with his heart in his eyes when he saw Violet in that vision of white lace and satin, the veil delicately covering her pretty face. He thought his heart might burst.

The ceremony was brief, poignant, and unforgettable. Blake lifted the veil to kiss his bride, and Violet's blue eyes brimmed over with tears as she returned the kiss with pure joy.

They walked out of the church into a soft rain of congratulations, confetti and rice.

"The rice is for fertility," Libby Collins whispered loudly.

"It worked!" Blake exclaimed in a stage whisper, with wicked eyes.

Violet whacked him with her bouquet and winked at Libby.

They climbed into the waiting limousine and sped away to Blake's house, to change clothes before the reception.

"What a good thing the reception isn't for another hour," Blake groaned as he kissed Violet hungrily in the big king-size bed.

"And you think we'll still make it in time? Optimist!" Violet panted, lifting up to the hard, measured thrust of his body.

He laughed, but the sensations caught him unaware and he arched, groaning with pleasure so deep it felt like pain.

Violet went with him, flying up into the sky like a rocket, exploding in sudden, fierce delight.

He increased the rhythm, and the pressure, and seconds later, he was right there with her, burning up in a fiery satisfaction that was vaguely shocking in its length. It seemed to go on forever.

When he was finally able to breathe again, he was wet with sweat and shaking all over. So was Violet.

"Wow," she whispered reverently as she met his eyes.

He nodded, bending to kiss her delicately. "See what a week of abstinence does to a normal man?" he murmured against her swollen lips.

"Want me to lock the bedroom door for a week to make it better…?" She jumped and cried out as he pinched her bottom.

He wrinkled his nose at her. "You lock it, I'll break it down," he challenged. "I hate abstinence!"

She wreathed her arms around his neck and smiled contentedly, although her heartbeat was still shaking her. She was wet with sweat, too, and working just to breathe.

"It's better every time," she said, dazed.

"I improve with practice," he informed her.

She grinned and slid her legs around his. "Do you, really? Let's see…!"

They knew the party was already underway before they got out of the shower. They dressed quickly in the clothing they'd laid out for the reception, a lacy pink dress for Violet and slacks with a white shirt, tie, and sports coat for Blake.

They were barely dressed, still smiling at each other in a daze of pleasure, when there was a loud rap on the front door.

They stared at each other. "Are we expecting anybody?" Blake asked curiously.

"I don't think so."

They went together to the front door and opened it.

Outside was most of the Jacobsville Police Department, with Chief Cash Grier, in uniform, leading the rest. He had a paper in his hand and he was grinning mischievously.

"Lady and gentleman," he began, "your friends in the Jacobsville Police Department would like to congratulate you on your recent nuptials and remind you that if you are ever in need of assistance, we are only as far away as your telephone. We have…"

"I'll call the governor!" Blake began, interrupting the speech.

Grier glared at him. "I have six pages to go."

"I have ten pages," Assistant Chief Judd Dunn announced, displaying them.

"I have a loaded shotgun," Blake told him.

Judd and Cash looked at each other speculatively. "How many years could he get if he pointed it at us?" Judd wondered aloud.

"That wouldn't be nice, on his wedding day," Cash agreed, but he gave Blake a rakish grin.

Blake's eyes narrowed. "Trespassing on private property," he began, "creating a public nuisance, terroristic threats and acts…"

"I am not a terrorist!" Cash informed him.

"But you are a public nuisance," Judd told Cash.

"Me?" Cash exclaimed.

Officer Dana Hall cleared her throat and elbowed both superior officers out of her way. She was holding a cake.

"This is the wedding cake from the reception," she told them, giving it to Violet. "I'm really sorry, but it was all we were able to save."

Violet was staring at her blankly.

Officer Hall cleared her throat. "Somebody spiked the

punch. Harden and Evan Tremayne drank it before they realized. One of the local cattlemen also drank some and made a very loud, unpleasant remark about lunatics who raised organic cattle just as Cy Parks walked in with J. D. Langley."

Cash cleared his throat. "Judd and I had to, sort of, shut down your wedding reception and lock up a few of your guests. But we saved your cake. There was some punch, too, but Officer Palmer there," he noted a tall, handsome blond officer with odd-colored highlights in his hair, "is wearing it."

Blake burst out laughing. Only in Jacobsville, he was thinking.

"Anyway, you're leaving right away on your honeymoon, right?" Judd asked them. "So you can get all the sandwiches and punch you want where you're going."

"Your jail is full, I guess?" Violet teased.

"Uh, yes it is, and he—" Cash indicated Blake "—represents Cy Parks and the Tremaynes. They want him to come down and get them out."

"That explains the cake," Blake told Violet.

She grinned at him. "We can detour through town on the way to the airport, can't we? After all, Mr. Parks did give me away."

"Good point." He sighed. "Okay, tell them I'm on the way. And, thanks for the cake."

"And the punch," Violet said with a glance at Palmer, who grinned back.

The police force got into its cars and left. Violet put the cake in the freezer. The house was quiet without Mee and Yow, who were being boarded for the honeymoon. Mrs. Hardy was staying at her house with a nurse.

"Would you like your wedding present now?" Blake asked as they were turning off the lights.

She turned and looked at him. "What is it?" she asked, surprised.

He pulled her close and kissed her. "Janet Collins cut a deal with the San Antonio D.A. She pled guilty for a reduced sentence, so there won't be a trial. You and your mother won't have the stress of a court trial."

"Oh, Blake!" She kissed him hungrily. "You had something to do with that, didn't you?"

He nodded, smiling. "I've been working on it for two weeks. It came through yesterday. I saved the news for today."

"Thank you," she said, and meant it fervently. She'd dreaded the idea of dredging the painful episode in public.

"I have to take care of my best girl," he whispered. "And the mother of my child." His big hand rested softly on her slightly swollen belly. "You were the most beautiful bride who ever walked down an aisle."

"And you were the handsomest groom." She kissed him back. "Well, shall we go and rescue some prominent local citizens on our way out of town?"

"Works for me," he chuckled.

They walked to the car hand in hand.

"Today is the first day of the rest of our lives," Blake mused.

"The rest of those days will be wonderful," she said softly. They were.

* * * * *

A new drama unfolds for
six of the state's wealthiest bachelors.

THE SECRET DIARY

This newest installment concludes with

A MOST SHOCKING REVELATION

by Kristi Gold

(Silhouette Desire, #1695)

Valerie Raines is determined to keep her mission
secret from Sheriff Gavin O'Neal. And that's easier
said than done when she's living in his house.
Especially when he's determined to seduce her!

*Available December 2005
at your favorite retail outlet.*

Tycoon Takes Revenge

by Anna DePalo

Infamous playboy Noah Whittaker gives gossip columnist Kayla Jones a taste of her own medicine, but will they find that love is far sweeter than revenge?

On sale
December 2005

Only from Silhouette Books.

If you enjoyed what you just read,
then we've got an offer you can't resist!

Take 2 bestselling
love stories FREE!
Plus get a FREE surprise gift!

Clip this page and mail it to Silhouette Reader Service™

IN U.S.A.
3010 Walden Ave.
P.O. Box 1867
Buffalo, N.Y. 14240-1867

IN CANADA
P.O. Box 609
Fort Erie, Ontario
L2A 5X3

YES! Please send me 2 free Silhouette Desire® novels and my free surprise gift. After receiving them, if I don't wish to receive anymore, I can return the shipping statement marked cancel. If I don't cancel, I will receive 6 brand-new novels every month, before they're available in stores! In the U.S.A., bill me at the bargain price of $3.80 plus 25¢ shipping and handling per book and applicable sales tax, if any*. In Canada, bill me at the bargain price of $4.47 plus 25¢ shipping and handling per book and applicable taxes**. That's the complete price and a savings of at least 10% off the cover prices—what a great deal! I understand that accepting the 2 free books and gift places me under no obligation ever to buy any books. I can always return a shipment and cancel at any time. Even if I never buy another book from Silhouette, the 2 free books and gift are mine to keep forever.

225 SDN DZ9F
326 SDN DZ9G

Name	(PLEASE PRINT)
Address	Apt.#
City	State/Prov. Zip/Postal Code

Not valid to current Silhouette Desire® subscribers.

Want to try two free books from another series?
Call 1-800-873-8635 or visit www.morefreebooks.com.

* Terms and prices subject to change without notice. Sales tax applicable in N.Y.
** Canadian residents will be charged applicable provincial taxes and GST.
  All orders subject to approval. Offer limited to one per household.
  ® are registered trademarks owned and used by the trademark owner and or its licensee.

DES04R

©2004 Harlequin Enterprises Limited

Trust Me

by Caroline Cross

Imprisoned on a tropical island by a ruthless dictator, aid worker Lilah Cantrell finds that her only hope for rescue is retrieval specialist Dominic Steele—the man who broke her heart years ago. But can she trust him to keep her safe...from him?

On sale
December 2005

Only from Silhouette Books.

COMING NEXT MONTH

#1693 NAME YOUR PRICE—Barbara McCauley
Dynasties: The Ashtons
His family's money and power tore them apart, but will time be able to heal the wounds of this priceless love?

#1694 TRUST ME—Caroline Cross
Men of Steele
An ex-navy SEAL is in over his head when he has to rescue the woman who broke his heart years ago.

#1695 A MOST SHOCKING REVELATION—Kristi Gold
Texas Cattleman's Club: The Secret Diary
A sexy sheriff is torn between his duty and his desire for a woman looking for her own brand of justice.

#1696 A BRIDE BY CHRISTMAS—Joan Elliott Pickart
Is this wedding planner really cursed never to find true love—or has Mr. Right just not appeared…until now?

#1697 TYCOON TAKES REVENGE—Anna DePalo
An infamous playboy gives a gossip columnist a taste of her own medicine, but finds that love is far sweeter than revenge.

#1698 TROPHY WIVES—Jan Colley
What will this wounded millionaire find beneath this rich girl's carefree facade?

SDCNM1105